MW00985287

MIKE HAMEL's MATTERHORN the BRAVE

No. 1

The Sword and the Flute

MIKE HAMEL's

MATTERHORN the BRAVE

No. 1

The Sword and the Flute

LIVING INK BOOKS
Writing Worth Reading

The Sword and the Flute
Matterhorn the Brave™ Series: Volume 1
Copyright © 2007 by Mike Hamel
Published by AMG Publishers
6815 Shallowford Rd.
Chattanooga, Tennessee 37421

All rights reserved. Except for brief quotations in printed reviews, no part of this publication may be reproduced, stored in a retrieval system or transmitted in any form or by any means (printed, written, photocopied, visual electronic, audio, or otherwise) without the prior permission of the publisher.

Published in association with the literary agency of Sanford Communications, Inc., 16778 S.E. Cohiba Ct., Damascus, OR 97089

MATTERHORN THE BRAVE is a trademark of CLW Communications Group, Inc.

ISBN: 978-089957833-0
First printing—January 2007
Cover designed by Daryle Beam, Chattanooga, Tennessee
Interior design and typesetting by Reider Publishing Services,
    West Hollywood, California
Edited and proofread by Pat Matuszak, Sharon Neal, Dan Penwell, and
    Rick Steele

Printed in Canada
13 12 11 10 09 08 07–T– 8 7 6 5 4 3 2 1

Library of Congress Cataloging-in-Publication Data

Hamel, Mike.
    The sword and the flute / Mike Hamel.
        p. cm. -- (Matterhorn the brave series ; v. 1)
    Previous ed. published: Colorado Springs, Colo. : Matterhorn Press, 2001, under the title *Ian's Flute*.
    Summary: When twelve-year-old Matthew Horn is transported into another realm by the Maker, he becomes Matterhorn the Brave, and, along with Aaron the Baron, must find the flute of Ian, the king of the leprechauns.
        ISBN-13: 978-0-89957-833-0 (pbk. : alk. paper)
        [1. Space and time--Fiction. 2. Christian life--Fiction. 3. Science fiction.]
    I. Hamel, Mike. Ian's flute. II. Title.
        PZ7.H176Swo 2007
        [Fic]--dc22
                                                    2006039358

The characters and stories in this series exist because of Susan, who made them all possible.

Contents

Introduction

A SAD thing happens to most people when they grow up. As their bodies get bigger, their imaginations get smaller. In time, their imaginations become so tiny and timid that they are afraid to go out alone. That's why kids have always been the greatest explorers. And among the greatest of them all are Matterhorn the Brave and his friends.

Matterhorn is a brave knight, when he isn't busy being a twelve-year-old boy.

Few people have heard of him, which isn't surprising, for most of his adventures happened in other times and places. And like all who know how to travel, he has learned to do so without drawing attention to himself. He and his friends have been around the globe and off it. Gone under the earth and over the moon. Not bad for kids who don't even have driver's licenses.

The books in this series don't reveal everything about this remarkable boy and his amazing companions. But herein are some of their greatest exploits for kids of all ages to enjoy. For Matterhorn is, after all, a twelve-year-old boy.

When he isn't busy being a brave knight.

Emerald Isle

A ARON the Baron hit the ground like a paratrooper, bending his knees, keeping his balance.
Matterhorn landed like a 210-pound sack of dirt.

His stomach arrived a few seconds later.

He straightened his six-foot-four frame into a sitting position. In the noonday sun he saw they were near the edge of a sloping meadow. The velvet grass was dotted with purple and yellow flowers. Azaleas bloomed in rainbows around the green expanse. The black-faced sheep mowing the far end of the field paid no attention to the new arrivals.

"Are you okay?" the Baron asked. He looked as if he'd just stepped out of a Marine recruiting poster. "We'll have to work on your landing technique."

"How about warning me when we're going somewhere," Matterhorn grumbled.

The Baron helped him up and checked his pack to make sure nothing was damaged. He scanned the landscape in all directions from beneath the brim of his red corduroy baseball cap. "It makes no difference which way we go," he said at last. "The horses will find us."

"What horses?"

"The horses that will take us to the one we came to see," the Baron answered.

"Are you always this vague or do you just not know what you're doing?"

"I don't know much, but I suspect this is somebody's field. We don't want to be caught trespassing. Let's go."

They left the meadow, walking single file through the tall azaleas up a narrow valley. Thorny bushes with loud yellow blossoms crowded the trail next to a clear brook. Pushing one of the prickly plants away, Matterhorn asked, "Do you know what these are?"

"Gorse, of course," the Baron said without turning.

"Never heard of it."

"Then I guess you haven't been to Ireland before."

"Ireland," Matterhorn repeated. "My great-grandfather came from Ireland."

"Your great-grandfather won't be born for centuries yet."

Matterhorn stepped over a tangle of exposed roots and said, "What do you mean?"

"I mean we're in medieval Ireland, not modern Ireland."

"How can that be?" Matterhorn cried, stopping in his tracks. "How can I be alive before my great-grandfather?"

The Baron shrugged. "That's one of the paradoxes of time travel. No one's been able to figure them all out.

You're welcome to try, but while you're at it, keep a lookout for the horses."

Matterhorn soon gave up on paradoxes and became absorbed in the paradise around him. The colors were so *alive* they hurt his eyes. He wished for a pair of sunglasses. Above the garish gorse he saw broom bushes and pine trees growing to the ridge where spectacular golden oaks crowned the slopes. Birdsongs whistled from their massive branches into the warm air. Small animals whispered in the underbrush while larger game watched the strangers from a distance.

The country flattened out and, at times, they glimpsed stone houses over the tops of hedgerows. They steered clear of these and any other signs of civilization. In a few hours, they reached the spring that fed the brook they had been following. They stopped to rest and wash up.

That's where the horses found them.

There were five strikingly handsome animals. The leader of the pack was from ancient and noble stock. He stood a proud seventeen hands high—five foot eight inches—at the shoulders. He had a classic Roman face with a white star on his wide forehead that matched the white socks on his forelegs. His straight back, sturdy body, and broad hindquarters suggested both power and speed. A rich coppery mane and tail complemented his sleek, chestnut coat.

The Baron held out an apple to the magnificent animal, but the horse showed no interest in the fruit or the man. Neither did the second horse. The third, a dappled stallion, took the apple and let the Baron pet his nose.

"These horses are free," the Baron said as he stroked the stallion's neck. "They choose their riders, which is as it should be. Grab an apple and find your mount."

While Matterhorn searched for some fruit, the leader sauntered over and tried to stick his big nose into Matterhorn's pack. When Matterhorn produced an apple, the horse pushed it aside and kept sniffing.

Did he want carrots, Matterhorn wondered? How about the peanut butter sandwich? Not until he produced a pocket-size Snickers bar did the horse whinny and nod his approval.

The Baron chuckled as Matterhorn peeled the bar and watched it disappear in a loud slurp. "That one's got a sweet tooth," he said.

The three other horses wandered off while the Baron and Matterhorn figured out how to secure their packs to the two that remained. "I take it we're riding without saddles or bridles," Matterhorn said. This made him nervous, as he had been on horseback only once before.

"Bridles aren't necessary," Aaron the Baron explained. "Just hold on to his mane and stay centered." He boosted Matterhorn onto his mount. "The horses have been sent for us. They'll make sure we get where we need to go."

As they set off, Matterhorn grabbed two handfuls of long mane from the crest of the horse's neck. He relaxed when he realized the horse was carrying him as carefully as if a carton of eggs were balanced on his back. Sitting upright, he said, "Hey, Baron! Check out this birthmark."

He rubbed a dark knot of tufted hair on the chestnut's right shoulder. "It looks like a piece of broccoli. I'm going to call him Broc."

"Call him what you want," the Baron said, "but you can't name him. The Maker gives the animals their names. A name is like a label; it tells you what's on the inside. Only the Maker knows that."

Much later, and miles farther into the gentle hills, they made camp in a lea near a tangle of beech trees. "You get some wood," the Baron said, "while I make a fire pit." He loosened a piece of hollow tubing from the side of his pack and gave it a sharp twirl. Two flanges unrolled outward and clicked into place to form the blade of a short spade. Next, he pulled off the top section and stuck it back on at a ninety-degree angle to make a handle.

Matterhorn whistled. "Cool!"

"Cool is what we'll be if you don't get going."

Matterhorn hurried into the forest. He was thankful to be alone for the first time since becoming an adult, something that had happened in an instant earlier that day. Seizing a branch, he did a dozen chin-ups then dropped and did fifty push-ups and a hundred sit-ups.

Afterward he rested against a tree trunk and encircled his right thigh with both hands. His fingertips didn't touch. Reaching farther down, he squeezed a rock-hard calf muscle.

All this bulk was new to him, yet it didn't feel strange. This was his body, grown up and fully developed. Flesh of his flesh; bone of his bone. Even hair of his hair, he thought, as he combed his fingers through the thick red ponytail.

He took the Sword hilt from his hip. The diamond blade extended and caught the late afternoon sun in a dazzling flash. This mysterious weapon was the reason he was looking for firewood in an Irish forest instead of sitting in the library at David R. Sanford Middle School.

The Call

Chapter 2

T HE Sword of Truth had called Matthew Horn on a
Friday afternoon.

As usual, he had finished his class work early and had
gone to the library. Miss Tull the librarian (everyone else
called her Miss Dull) glanced up from her book, pleased
to see him. Matt spent a lot of time down here reading
or drawing or just sitting, his green eyes half closed under
a shock of unruly hair. He didn't have as many freckles
as most redheads, but enough to give his full face some
character.

Matt was big for his age, an early bloomer nearing
six feet tall. The growth spurt made him a bit clumsy, but
who isn't at twelve? His friends called him Big Red. His
teachers called him "precocious," which means too
smart, too young. They talked about him skipping a
grade next year. Fine with Matt. That would put him a
year closer to high school and a shot at their powerhouse
soccer and wrestling teams. His older brother Victor was
an All-State wrestling champ who always practiced on

9

Matt. As a result, Matt could pin much larger and older opponents. He was anxious to follow in his brother's footsteps, now that Vic had gone off to college.

The library was Matt's favorite part of David R. Sanford Middle School. Located in the basement underneath the cafeteria, the huge room smelled of old books and cold pizza. Solid oak tables with initials scarred into their faces and petrified gum caked onto their bellies lounged around the main room. Gray metal bookshelves poked out in all directions, each ending in a study carrel. Matt's favorite happened to be in the farthest corner from the librarian's desk.

He dropped his backpack by his chair and rummaged through it in search of *A Connecticut Yankee in King Arthur's Court*. Like most of the books Mrs. Williams assigned, this one was good enough to read a second time. What he pulled out instead was *A Study in Scarlet*, the book that had introduced him, and the world, to Sherlock Holmes.

Replacing the dog-eared volume, he felt the tiny bottle of insanity sauce he used to spice up the school lunches. The potent seasoning had gotten him into trouble a few weeks earlier when he let a curious buddy try some. The poor kid howled loud enough to bring the principal.

In most cases Mr. Hatcher would have tossed the sauce—end of story. But he realized the incident had been an accident. He also had a taste for the fiery, and he admitted that the tired menu needed serious help. He returned the hot sauce on condition that Matt never share it with mere mortals again.

Matt's gaze wandered over to Mr. Rickets. Mr. Rickets was an antique bookshelf donated to the school years ago when the town library had been remodeled. He came stocked with several strange and curious volumes. Since Miss Tull never met a book she didn't like, she refused to throw any of them away. Those that were too old or odd to associate with the other books, she left with Mr. Rickets.

Some old furniture is warm and friendly like a favorite uncle. Mr. Rickets was weird and decrepit like a hobo. Cobweb hair sprouted from his top shelf. A musty smell clung to him like cheap cologne. His sagging shelves held tired books suffering from bad backs and loose joints. One volume stuck out from the center shelf, its shiny gold lettering out of place on the wrinkled leather skin.

Why hadn't he noticed that one before, Matt wondered? He walked over and tried to hip the book back into place.

It wouldn't budge.

Matt had strong legs. His goalie kicks often sailed past midfield. He pushed harder.

Nothing happened.

He bent down and shoved, putting his shoulder into it. Still the book wouldn't go in.

The harder he pushed the madder he got. Swatting the stubborn hardback in frustration, he saw it jiggle forward.

If it won't go in, maybe it would come out. He yanked it free—and promptly dropped it on the floor, creating a small cloud of dust.

The book was thick as a brick and heavier than Matt expected. He lugged it to his carrel, anxious to find out what made it so weighty. Blowing off the remaining dust, he opened the cover.

The words on the title page matched those on the spine.

The Sword and the Flute.

No author.

No publisher.

No copyright date.

No other information appeared on any page. It seemed completely blank.

Matt tugged at the hair behind his left ear, a sign that his brain had gone into overdrive. Next in motion were his feet, as he went to ask Miss Tull about the peculiar book. She wasn't at her desk, so he checked the computer and the old card catalog. *The Sword and the Flute* wasn't listed.

It was five minutes until three when he returned to his carrel and began flipping through the blank pages. Although paper-thin, they had the weight of hammered metal. Their gilded edges cast slivers of light as they pranced from right to left.

Matt stopped in the exact middle of the book. On the left-hand page was a black dot the size of a period. As he stared, it seemed to be coming toward him like the snout of a slow-moving train. The sound of a distant wind grew with the optical illusion.

He squirmed in his seat as the oncoming mystery reached half a page in size. The 3-D effect gave the sensation of staring into a bottomless well. He could now see that the void was whirring, spiraling inward. Air whistled by his ears and down the hole.

It made him think of the black holes his Uncle Al often spoke about.

Some physicists thought they might be wormholes in space through which matter could travel to distant parts of the universe. Of course, this couldn't be a *real* black hole because its enormous gravity would have swallowed him, the school, and the whole town without so much as a burp.

Matt rubbed his eyes. This couldn't be happening! He was just tired from the long practices for the Park District soccer championship this weekend. His eyes and ears were playing tricks; his fingers would tell the truth, though. Cautiously he reached for the black circle.

As he touched the page his hand disappeared, followed by his arm. He felt like a lump of dough being stretched into molecule-thin spaghetti. There was no pain, just a fizzing sensation as his body dissolved.

His vision blurred and faded to black.

His pulse raced, then froze.

Static.

Silence.

First Realm

THE next thing Matt knew he was skittering across the floor of a dimly lit room about the size of the school gym. The echoing in his ears resolved itself into a persistent "here . . . ere . . . re."

"Herere."

"Here."

"Come here."

When Matt's eyes adjusted, he saw a young woman seated on a stage about ten yards away. Everything from the crown on her head to the throne on which she sat said she was royalty!

"I do not bite," the woman said. "Come here."

He rose slowly and obeyed.

A quick smile crossed her face but didn't seem to reach her light brown eyes, which took his measure. A gold crown studded with fire opals floated on layers of milk chocolate hair. Her blue satin gown spilled over her shoulders like a waterfall. The fabric was a shade lighter than the large sapphire sparkling at her neck. A lion-headed charm bracelet encircled her left wrist, from which dangled a half dozen elegantly carved animals. She was the very picture of calm beauty.

Except for the Sword in her lap.

Matt's jaw dropped at the sight of the blade. It was made of a single diamond, three feet long. In its center glowed a thread of light like a frozen sunbeam.

"Beautiful, is it not?" the woman said. "It is the Sword of Truth. You are the knight it has called. I am Queen Bea of First Realm. What is your name?"

Matt was speechless.

"We do not have all day," Bea said.

"I'm Matthew Horn," he finally managed.

When he spoke, a pulse flashed through the blade. The stabbing brightness filled his vision with pinwheels and made his eyes water.

"Welcome to First Realm, Matterhorn," Bea said, running his name together.

Matt scanned his memory for any reference to First Realm while he squinted into the gloom for clues to his whereabouts. There were no windows offering an outside view, no doors, no clocks, no pictures. The library smell was gone, replaced by a hint of peppermint.

"I've never heard of First Realm," Matt said at last, taking a cautious step toward the seated woman.

"There is much you humans have never heard of," Bea said, pushing the footstool away from the throne. "Your race is quite ignorant when it comes to traveling."

"You humans," Matt repeated to himself. What did that make her?

"So few of you bother to go beyond," Bea continued. "The curious among you become philosophers or mystics or physicists. Yet, even they seldom travel."

"We travel a lot," Matt countered. "We've got cars and planes and ships. We've even been to the moon. But you'd know that if you were from Earth, which," he added carefully, "I take it you're not."

"No I am not," Bea replied.

"Are you an alien?"

"Actually, you are the alien here."

"Where is *here*?"

"The Propylon in First Realm."

How had he gone from the library at school to someplace he'd never heard of? Then it came to him: he must be daydreaming. This royal fantasy sprang from his recent reading. In *A Connecticut Yankee,* Hank Morgan had been transported to Camelot by a blow on the head. Matt reached up to check his forehead—and stared at the forearm in front of his face.

It was hairy and muscular.

Looking down, he saw a different body from the one he had taken to school that morning. His eyes were four inches higher from the floor. His arms and legs were bigger, thicker. Even his jeans and sweatshirt had grown. His hair had stretched into a ponytail resting between his shoulder blades. The journey here had aged him to adulthood. He had hyper-jumped over puberty, pimples, and the prom.

"In the place where you live," Bea explained, "life unfolds gradually. A tree has to mature before you can eat its fruit. A rose must bloom before you can enjoy its fragrance. This process does not apply when you become a Traveler. What you will become, you already are."

The drastic change scared and excited Matt at the same time. He sensed the latent strength in his new muscles. He flexed his biceps and felt the bulge under his sleeve. If only he could take this body to the wrestling mat, or the soccer pitch, and try it out!

"You will be able to use your new muscles soon enough," Bea said. "More importantly, you will have the chance to use this." Rising with the Sword in both hands, she glided forward, preceded by the scent of jasmine. The hem of her gown swept the purple carpet as she strode between the sleek alabaster urns by the stairs.

"When the Maker created First Realm," she said from an arm's length away, "He established a royal family to teach His law, administer His justice, and preserve His peace."

"Sounds like you're talking about God," Matt said. "Why do you call him the Maker?"

"Because that is what He is. Your word 'God' is an empty noun. It needs definition. But 'Maker' is an active verb, full of meaning. It describes the One who expanded time-space and created energy-matter. He is Lord of the past, the present, and the possible.

"The Sword of Truth is one of the Ten Talis the Maker fashioned to help us rule," Bea said with a nod to the diamond shaft. "They are tokens of His nature, reminders of who He is. Each has power in keeping with what it represents. The Sword symbolizes the Maker's truthfulness. Its light exposes deception."

"Fascinating," Matt said, not taking his eyes from the Sword. "But I still don't know what all this has to do with me."

"You'll find out soon enough," said the stranger who appeared in a doorway to Matt's left.

The Baron

THE six-foot-three newcomer wore faded jeans and a light gray T-shirt. A red corduroy baseball cap rested on buzz-cut hair the color of toast. His piercing, blue-gray eyes seemed to take in everything at once. A square chin gave a confident cast to his tanned face. His wide shoulders tapered to a slim waist.

Now this is the kind of man who could handle the Sword, Matt thought as the stranger approached. My being here is a mistake.

Bea made the introductions. "Matterhorn, this is Aaron the Baron. He is also a Traveler and a friend of the Realm."

"Yell-O," Matt said in his personal slang. "And it's Matthew Horn, not Matterhorn." He stuck out his hand, but Aaron the Baron ignored it and put his left hand on Matt's left shoulder by way of greeting.

Turning to the Queen, he asked, "Where's Princess Jewel?"

"I have not been able to reach her," Bea said. "While I was trying, the Sword summoned Matterhorn. He will have to do."

Matt had no idea why he was here, but he didn't appreciate being talked about like leftover meat loaf. "Do for what?" he demanded.

"To help in the lost and found department," the Baron said, as if that explained everything.

As daydreams go, this one was getting more and more weird. School should be over by now. Why hadn't the bell awakened him? Matt pointed to Bea. "She thinks I'm a knight, but I'm not."

"Knight or no, it is time to go," Bea said, smiling at her rhyme. "The Baron can fill you in on the details."

"Leave!" Matt protested. "I just got here. What did you call this place, the Propy-what?"

"Propylon," Bea said. "Also known as the Hall of Portals. Think of it as an airport. Travelers use it to go wherever they want."

"Airports are a lot busier than this," Matt said, glancing around.

"Well, more like a private jet port," Bea said. "Few people have access to the Propylon. It is the most important place in First Realm. There are many portals through time-space, but this is the only portal hub in the multiverse. You can visit almost anywhere from here, including the past."

As she spoke, the Queen made a slight gesture with one hand and the lighting in the room went up. So did Matt's eyebrows. Rich tapestries of burgundy and gold and hunter green covered the walls from floor to vaulted ceiling. Potted trees and ferns flourished everywhere, giving the place the texture of an indoor garden. A miniature forest of peppermint plants accounted for the air's freshness.

The platform beneath the Queen's throne was a circular slab of rose quartz three feet high. The throne itself rested on four eagle claws, each grasping a different colored gem the size of a softball. Crisp reds and cerulean blues danced inside the opals studding its arms and legs. Plush crimson cushions padded the seat and back.

"This is the Royal Chamber," Bea said with a sweep of her arm. "It is one of the Propylon's many rooms."

A dozen questions tried to bungee jump off Matt's tongue. Before any of them got past his lips, Aaron the Baron said, "I can explain more on the way. Grab the Sword and let's go. We have to see a horse about a man."

Matt hesitated. "Do I have a choice?" he asked.

"Yes, Matterhorn," Bea said. "Those who serve the Maker do so of their own free will." She pointed at the wall behind him. Through a circular opening, Matt could see the school library and the bookshelves near his carrel.

"Return to your world if you wish," Bea offered. "The Sword will summon another worthy to wield it." Then, with a challenge in her voice, she added, "Or, you can follow your destiny."

Dream or no, it was decision time. Return to being Matt the kid, or go forward as Matterhorn the Knight—at least for a few minutes. How could he go back when he had the chance to go exploring!

With a shiver of excitement he said, "I'll take that Sword now."

Queen Bea extended the weapon. "This is different from any sword you have used before."

"You can say that again," Matt muttered. The most lethal weapon he owned was a pocketknife.

"Let me show you something," Bea said, handing him the Sword.

Matt was surprised at how light, yet solid, it felt. The red leather hilt adjusted to his hand and seemed to be gripping him instead of the other way around. He felt a slight pulsing. Cautiously he swished the blade from side to side.

"How old are you?" Bea asked casually.

"Twelve," Matt answered, fighting off an invisible attacker.

"Are you an honest young man? Do you always tell the truth?"

"Yes, ma'am," Matt said. A brilliant pain zinged up his right arm as if he'd stuck the tip of the Sword into a light socket. He dropped the weapon and yelped. The unexpected jolt almost knocked him off his feet.

You weren't supposed to feel pain in dreams, Matt thought.

"Pick up the Sword," Bea said. It was a command, not a request. "Never forget, this is the Sword of Truth. You cannot hold it and speak a lie. You do not have to be perfect to use it—only its Maker is perfect—but you do need to be honest."

Matt gingerly retrieved the Sword. He noticed something engraved in flowing script on the silver crosspiece: *Truth is a Blade sharp as Light.*

"A moment ago, I said you had a choice," Bea continued. "Always remember that it is a *second* choice, for the Maker has first chosen you. It is a high calling. If you serve well, you will serve long."

"Why me?" Matt wanted to know.

Queen Bea sighed. "I am not sure. This has never happened before, a Talis summoning a human. But I can tell you this; there must be something special about you that suits the Sword. Are you prepared to swear allegiance to its Maker?"

A half hour ago, Matthew Horn had never heard of First Realm or the Sword of Truth. Now these things seemed as real as anything he had ever experienced. He read the hope on the Queen's face and the questions in the Baron's eyes. He felt the mystery and power of this unusual weapon. The thought of where it might take him filled him with energy—and dread.

Tightening his grip on the hilt with both hands, he said, "I'm ready."

Sword Sworn

Chapter 5

Q UEEN Bea nodded. "Do you solemnly swear to
follow where the Sword of Truth leads and to
faithfully serve its Maker?"

"I do," Matterhorn replied.

"To the death?" the Queen asked.

Matterhorn paused. What was he getting himself
into? He glanced back at the school library through the
circular opening in the wall. He looked down at the
Sword. This was a weapon in his hands, not a violin
bow. And his body was now big enough to do some serious damage with it if he had to. But "to the death"
seemed over the top.

The Queen waited for his answer.

"I'll do my best," was all Matterhorn could manage.

The blade flashed, sealing the bargain between man
and Talis. Queen Bea smiled. "Good enough. Have faith
in the Sword and stay close to the Baron. You can trust
both with your life." Under her breath she added, "As
you may soon discover."

Turning to Aaron the Baron, she said, "These are desperate times. It is important that you find what you seek. Be careful with your toys. And do not teach the locals anything they should not know. You must limit the changes you cause."

"I know, Your Majesty," the Baron replied. In a quieter tone he added, "Sorry about your father."

The Queen's shoulders stiffened and she closed her eyes for a long moment. When she opened them she asked, "Are you two still here?"

"Just leaving," the Baron said with a bow.

"Will I see you again?" Matterhorn asked.

"I hope so. Serve well."

"Serve long," Aaron the Baron replied. He led Matterhorn through the doorway that opened onto a narrow corridor with off-white walls and light blue carpeting. "We have to stop by my place for a few things," he explained, veering right at the end of the hall.

Matterhorn followed the red baseball cap into a larger passageway. As they hurried along, he noticed doors of varying shapes and sizes. Some were guarded by granite-faced men. The air around them crackled with such power that the hair all over Matterhorn's body came to attention. The tall figures wore loose-fitting cassocks belted with different colored sashes. None carried weapons; yet they had the unmistakable aura of being dangerous.

The Baron paused to speak with one silver-sashed guard. "Any word about your captain, Trayko?"

"No," Trayko replied.

"Any idea what happened?"

Trayko looked at Matterhorn and didn't answer.

"Next time," the Baron said and started walking.

"What was that about?" Matterhorn asked when they were out of earshot.

"Realm business," he answered mysteriously.

"What's behind all these doors?"

"I've only been in a few rooms myself, but I assume they're full of portals like the one you came through." Pointing right with his chin, the Baron said, "The Earth Room is that way." Then he took a sharp left down an empty hallway, halting in front of a normal-looking door. "This is where I stay when I'm here," he said, placing his right hand on a palm reader. "It's my shop."

As the door swung open, Matterhorn saw work-benches sticking out of three walls like fat tongues from pimply, pegboard faces. Piles of old magazines and technical journals were crammed beneath the benches. The hum of computers and the purr of electrical motors created a soothing background music.

On the workbench opposite the door sat a laptop computer hooked to an oversized flat screen monitor. Cabling snaked everywhere among the odd assortment of devices. Stacks of storage discs formed a skyline to the techno-scape. Electronic gear, scopes, and small machines crowded the other benches, along with tools and a few dirty plates. A thin smell of oil coated the air.

"Where'd you get all this stuff?" Matterhorn asked the back of the Baron's head as he followed his host upstairs.

"Brought most of it from home; picked up the rest on my travels. A lot of the scopes I built myself. I like to tinker around and make things. If you're hungry," he said, changing the subject, "you can make us some macaroni and cheese while I finish packing." He steered Matterhorn to a cozy kitchen. "But be quick, we need to leave soon."

Mac-and-cheese wasn't high on Matterhorn's list of favorite foods, but he was hungry. Waiting for the water to boil, he watched Aaron the Baron cram two old backpacks full of foodstuffs, antique cooking utensils, bedrolls, and other supplies, including a first-aid kit stenciled with a red cross. The fabric packs had no frames, just sturdy shoulder straps. Along their tops and sides ran strips of shiny metallic tape. A rubbery yellow lining covered their backsides.

"Come and get it!" Matterhorn shouted when the food was ready.

The Baron walked into the kitchen holding a couple of square patches.

"What are those?"

"Scritch pads. I developed the material myself."

"They look like Velcro."

"Same idea, but these are much stronger."

"What are they for?"

"You can't walk around with that Sword in your hand all the time. You're liable to cut somebody's ear off, and I don't want it to be mine." Using goop from a tiny tube, he stuck one pad to Matterhorn's belt and the other to the Sword hilt.

"Very clever," Matterhorn said. "But what about a sheath for the blade?"

"What blade?" the Baron asked, giving the handle back to Matterhorn.

The diamond shaft was gone. The crosspiece had also retracted into the hilt. "What happened?" Matterhorn asked.

"Travel mode," the Baron said.

Matterhorn stared at the red hilt with its silver pommel. "It's like a light saber."

"Far from it," the Baron replied. "The blade's not made of energy, but of the hardest substance in the universe. Besides, light sabers aren't real; the Sword of Truth is." He pointed to the pad and said, "Stick the hilt on your belt."

Matterhorn did so.

"Now try to pull it off."

He couldn't. Even with his adult strength he was unable to separate the two pieces of scritch.

Aaron smiled. "Here's the secret of scritch. Pull downward from the right to the left like peeling a banana."

Matterhorn tried it and the patches came apart with a soft, scritching sound.

"Hence, the name," the Baron said, obviously pleased with himself. "Now, let's eat."

Costume Party

BETWEEN bites of macaroni, the Baron asked Matterhorn how he had gotten to the Propylon.

"I wish I knew," Matterhorn replied. "I found this strange book in the library at school. I got sucked into it like a piece of string into a vacuum cleaner. The next thing I know, I'm lying on the floor at the feet of a queen."

The Baron nodded knowingly. "You were digitized and posted."

"What's that mean?"

"You were broken down into energy packets, sent here, and reassembled."

Matterhorn scowled.

"Do you know much about the Internet?"

"Some."

"The Propylon is like a router on the Net," the Baron mumbled through a mouthful of food. "It's a node in the zero-point energy field of time-space."

"Time-space?"

"The fabric of the multiverse," the Baron said. "Anyway, information can move through the Propylon trans-dimensionally. All matter, including us, is made of energy and energy can be zipped around like Email."

"People aren't Email!"

"Energy is energy."

"What you're implying is impossible."

Aaron the Baron reached over and poked Matterhorn in the arm with his fork.

"Ouch!" Matterhorn cried. "Why'd you do that?"

"To prove this isn't a dream, which is what you've been telling yourself."

Just then, a mechanical voice squawked from the laptop on the bench below. "Incoming. Incoming."

"That's a priority Email," the Baron said. He jumped from the table and descended the stairs, three at a time, to his workbench.

"You can get Email here?" Matterhorn asked as he trailed along at a more cautious pace.

"I figured a way to keep a virtual link open to my home computer," Aaron said, pulling up a chair and sitting on it backward.

Matterhorn looked over the Baron's shoulder. The Email read:

Hi Baron, I wish I could come with you, but my mom isn't doing well. She starts another round of chemotherapy tomorrow, and I can't leave her. I realize time is relative when traveling, and I wouldn't be gone that long. But you and I both

*know the possibility of not returning from these
trips. I can't risk that now. I hope you understand. Maybe next time.*

Jewel

"That's disappointing," the Baron said. "We could
use her help, but family comes first."

"Is this the princess that you and the Queen were
talking about?"

"Yeah. Want to see her picture?" He double-clicked
a file on the desktop.

The first features Matterhorn noticed, as the pixels
arranged themselves into a female face, were the liquid
brown eyes. Innocent and open, they beamed from an
oval face as smooth as satin. The young woman had a
cinnamon complexion and brunette hair that poured
over her right shoulder in a thick braid. Her perfectly
matched teeth were framed by full lips.

"She's pretty," Matterhorn said. "What did she mean
about not returning?"

"Traveling is risky business," the Baron replied. "No
telling what kind of mess we might land in."

"Could we be hurt?"

The Baron nodded as he closed the file.

"Killed?"

"Yeah. Still want to go?"

Matterhorn was having second thoughts.

"You don't have anything to worry about," Aaron
reassured him, "as long as you've got the Sword."

"I'm not sure how much good it will do me," Matterhorn said, drawing the hilt with difficulty from his belt. The diamond blade extended. "I don't know the first thing about using a sword."

The Baron crossed to the other side of the room. He pulled a Chinese throwing star from a pocket on his thigh and flung the deadly disk at Matterhorn's head.

Quicker than Matterhorn could think, the Sword sliced upward to deflect the star. The second and third stars came just as fast, but fared no better.

The Baron walked over and picked up the lethal weapons.

Matterhorn shivered, and shook the instant sweat from his brow. Those mini saw blades could have ripped his face open. The clang of them bouncing off the Sword still rang in his ears.

"Don't take it personally," the Baron said. "I'm fast, but nothing can get past that blade. You're safer with that in your hands than if you were inside a tank."

"Why didn't you warn me!" Matterhorn almost screamed.

"And miss the expression on your face?" Aaron opened a closet beneath the stairway and rummaged among hangers of old clothes. "Put these on," he said, tossing Matterhorn a pair of woolen pants and a linen shirt with full sleeves. Neither article had buttons or zippers.

Matterhorn removed his shirt, pulled the linen one over his head, and laced the neck ties. He changed pants and threaded his belt through the loops in the waistband. Then he reattached the hilt to the scritch pad. Lastly, he shifted the contents of his pockets to his new clothes.

He carried two items at all times. The first was a small blue notebook with a yellow golf pencil stabbed through its wire spine. He wrote down memorable sayings he read or heard in this quote book until he could transfer them to the master file on his computer. The second item was a harmonica he'd taught himself to play.

Aaron changed into similar clothes, except that his pants had more pockets. He handed Matterhorn a fleece vest and a pair of supple leather boots. "These are the biggest shoes I have, size twelve. See if they'll work."

Matterhorn sat in the hammock chair suspended in the corner and tried them on. They were a bit tight, but soft enough that they might stretch. "They'll do," he said as he stood. "Why the costumes?"

Handing Matterhorn a pack, the Baron replied, "For the same reason we're using these old things instead of modern gear. To blend in. Travelers must never draw attention to themselves. Put your clothes in your pack. With any luck, you won't be returning here."

Matterhorn obeyed. "You still haven't told me where we're going."

Aaron the Baron smiled. "I'll show you. Come here."

Matterhorn stepped closer and studied the rounded object in the Baron's left hand. It looked like an old-fashioned Rubik's cube with partially melted sides. Each facet was a different gemstone. The glimmering colors swirled together in a bizarre way that made Matterhorn dizzy when he tried to focus on it.

The Baron carefully placed his fingers around the deformed globe like a pitcher searching for the seams before throwing a fastball. After a final adjustment he gave the gizmo a sharp twist.

The floor disappeared and the duo dropped into a field in Ireland.

Pint-Sized Potentate

A ND that was how Matterhorn came to be where he was now, looking for firewood in a forest so overgrown and snarled that it took him a while to fill his arms with sticks. He had a pretty good sense of direction, but he could see how someone might easily get lost in this place. Retracing his steps, he found Aaron tending a small fire in a shallow, rock-rimmed circle.

"What took you so long?" the Baron asked.

"Daydreaming," Matterhorn replied. He glanced around the clearing and asked uneasily, "Where are the horses?"

"Relax. They'll be back if we need them. Let's eat."

Dinner turned out to be the low point of Matterhorn's day. The Baron's stew was thin and murky as pond water. Whatever meat and vegetables had been used were boiled beyond recognition. The toasted cheese sandwiches tasted like pieces of charcoal glued together with orange paste. This fare was worse than anything Matterhorn had eaten at the school cafeteria. If only he had some insanity sauce to spice things up.

After supper the Baron threw wispy clumps of moss into the fire. The resulting smoke stung Matterhorn's eyes. "What'd you do that for?" he asked.

"It keeps the bugs away," the Baron said, sipping on a tin mug of steaming cocoa.

Matterhorn moved back a few feet and took out his harmonica. It looked so small in his large hands. He had been twelve years old the last time he'd played it—only one day ago! He moistened his lips and started into a Dixieland riff. Soon his foot was tapping with the tune and his worries were dissolving in the one-two rhythm.

Several songs later, he finished playing, but the music didn't stop. A vocal descant floated in on the evening breeze. The answering tune grew louder until the singer followed his melody into the clearing.

Clad in a pine green coat, earth-tone britches and pointy shoes, a man about eighteen inches tall appeared out of the dusk. The startled campers leapt to their feet. The Baron touched his forehead and bowed.

The visitor touched his hat with his stout walking stick and nodded back. "Are ye the Tall Ones I'm to be expectin'?" he said in a high-pitched voice.

This squeaky stranger sounded like he'd been breathing helium, and Matterhorn stifled a laugh. A moment later he struggled not to cry out when the man thwacked him on the shins with the blackthorn walking stick that doubled as a weapon.

Wow, that hurt! Matterhorn hopped around rubbing one leg, then the other. He could feel dents in his shin-bones.

"Great snort!" the little man bellowed. "Where be yer manners, ye lout?" Anger flushed the chubby cheeks on either side of his bulbous nose. Fiery green eyes flashed beneath shaggy brows.

"Your pardon," Aaron the Baron said. "This is our first time in Ireland. Would you be Ian, king of the leprechauns?"

"In the province of Connacht, I'd be," the stranger answered.

"Leprechauns!" Matterhorn cried. "You mean the fairy tales and legends are true?"

"Legends are the cotton candy that gets spun around a stick of truth," Aaron quipped.

That's a good quote for my book, Matterhorn thought.

"Ian is a direct descendant of the Sidhe, of the race Tuatha," the Baron added.

"And worthy of a wee bit of respect," the pint-sized potentate said, folding his arms across his chest. The king's ears stuck through his curly sideburns and matched the color of his red felt cap. His skin was bunched and wrinkled as though there was too much of it to fit on his face. Above his right eye bloomed a large purple mole sprouting a single gray hair.

Matterhorn tried not to stare. "I'm sorry, Your Highness," he apologized. "I meant no disrespect."

"*Highness!*" the leprechaun screeched. "Do I look like a *High*-ness?" He raised his stick and Matterhorn twisted sideways to avoid another blow.

That's when Ian saw the Sword. The blade had extended and a thin sliver of light glowed through its center. The leprechaun lowered his staff.

"Forgive me temper, sir. I see from the Sword that ye be the Queen's knight. She said you'd come."

The Baron's forehead wrinkled at this. "The Queen's been here?"

"In a dream, sir. The day after me flute was stolen."

"Have a seat and tell us what happened," the Baron invited. "Would you like some hot chocolate?"

The mini monarch perched on a rock near the fire. He laid his staff, known as a shillelagh, across his lap. "What kind of spirits be hot chocolate?" he asked warily.

"It's not spirits Your High—, I mean Your Grace."

Good recovery, Matterhorn thought, still rubbing his shins.

"Chocolate is a confection," the Baron said. "A flavor. It makes a great drink. Here, try some." He handed Ian the battered tin cup, which the leprechaun took by the rim so as not to burn his fingers. After a big sniff he tried a small sip. His eyebrows wiggled in delight. He took another swig, then another, until the dark liquid was gone.

"'Great Peep, 'tis delightful!" he exclaimed. "Might I have another draft?"

Aaron refilled Ian's cup. He noticed the age spots on the leprechaun's hands and the white hair around the bracelet of amber beads and wondered how old Ian was. "What can you tell us about your flute?" he asked.

The king put down his cocoa to let it cool. He drew a smooth stick on a leather cord from around his neck. "The Flute's been in me family for generations," he explained. "I got it from me father on his deathbed. He got it from me grandfather, who got it from his. A few weeks ago, I woke to find this in its place. A piece of wood where the silver rod had been."

"Is that why someone's stolen it?" Matterhorn interrupted. "Because it's silver?"

The Baron answered before Ian could. "Probably not. It's far more valuable than the metal it's made of. Like the Sword you carry, Ian's Flute is a Talis from First Realm. It was entrusted to the leprechauns for safekeeping."

Ian nodded at the Baron's words and kept his head down in shame at having failed his sacred duty.

Matterhorn laid more wood on the fire. After an awkward silence, he asked, "Is the Flute named after you?"

Ian retrieved his chocolate and took a loud swig. "I'm named fer the Flute," he replied, "not t' other way round. The Tall Ones hereabouts call it the Pixie Piccolo, but the gentleman who gave it t' me ancestors called it Ian's Flute. Said 'twas named after the greatest musician ever to play it."

"The Queen told me the Talis have special powers," Matterhorn went on. "What does the Flute do?"

Bonehand

KING Ian took a pipe from his coat pocket. He stuffed shredded leaves into the bowl carved from a giant acorn and scratched a match on his boot heel. He blew blackberry-scented smoke rings into the night and, with a faraway look, began his story.

"If I had the Flute t' play now, ye'd hear nothin' more than if I blew on this pipe," he said. "Only the rarest and shyest creatures can hear the music. And when they hear it, oh, they can't help but come to the sonorous sound, so transported with joy that they'll do whate'er the player asks.

"I've played the Flute fer unicorns and watched those wondrous creatures dance on moonbeams. I've played it on the coast and seen the pleasure of the white dolphins caperin' in the surf. What a joy 'tis to give joy."

"Why would anyone want to steal it?" Matterhorn wondered aloud.

"Because of its pow'r," Ian said, surprised the lad didn't grasp the obvious. "In the wrong hands, it'll do great harm. Unicorns could be lured into traps; their horns cut off and ground into sorcerer's potions. White dolphins could be drawn into nets and filleted alive. Their flesh is a great delicacy.

"But that's not why the Flute was snatched," the king continued, his eyelids dropping to half-mast. "I fear something worse. Something ye may be too late t' stop." His concern hung wreathed in a cloud of gloomy smoke.

"We'll do all we can to find the Flute," the Baron spoke up.

As if in agreement, the Sword at Matterhorn's side pulsed brightly. Then the blade retracted. Matterhorn wondered what Sherlock Holmes would do with a case like this. Look for a trail of clues, no doubt. But where to begin?

Ian puffed through his acorn of tobacco and refilled his pipe. "I've had me people goin' through these woods like bees through an orchard," he continued. "We've got nothin' t' show fer our trouble. I'm afraid all I can tell ye is the thief's name."

"You *know* who stole the Flute!" the Baron cried, spilling his chocolate.

"That I do," Ian sighed. "He used t' be me friend. His name is Bonehand."

"What kind of name is *Bonehand*?"

"Well, it ain't his given name," Ian admitted, "but 'tis what everyone calls him now. Walk a bit and I'll tell ye the story, fer I must be on me way." He tapped out his pipe and put it away, then pulled himself up by his shillelagh.

The Baron and Matterhorn accompanied Ian along a winding path southward from the clearing. The sun had grown tired of eavesdropping and had fallen asleep behind the heather hills. The moon peeked over the east horizon, not sure it was safe to rise and shine.

"Ye must be wary of Bonehand," Ian warned his long-legged companions. "But ye should also know that he wasn't always bad. Life's dealt him many a cruel blow. His parents died in a fire when he weren't no bigger 'n me. The lad hid in the woods to keep from being sent t' his auntie in England. The Tall Ones searched fer days and never found him. They gave 'im up fer dead.

"But he was a survivor, that boy. Only had to see a thing done once t' figure out how t' do it himself. He became wiser in the ways of nature than most animals. We met in the forest while he was still a youth. We often sat by the fire and talked. I watched him grow up bear-strong and fox-sly."

The king's voice held a tone of respect as he told his tale. But there was also a raw edge of pain caused by Bonehand's suspected betrayal.

Ian stopped walking, but kept talking. "Bonehand never returned t' his people. Instead, he made himself the Warden of the Woods that stretch from the hills t' the sea. He loves the animals and has become their protector. One spring a few years ago, some soldiers came. They killed many animals fer sport, leaving carcasses t' rot in the sun. They set fire t' the trees just t' watch 'em burn. They made a game of racing the flames on their swift steeds. But they couldn't outrun the Warden. None of 'em made it out of the woods alive."

The leprechaun shivered with the memory and began moving again. "The Warden saved many an animal that day, including a stag trapped under a flaming tree. In the process his right hand was so badly burned he should ha' lost it. Yet he scraped away the dead flesh and left the bones and tendons. In time, he taught himself t' use that hand again. 'Tis the scariest thing ye ne'er want t' see.

"The fire changed the man in other ways," Ian went on. "His mood became darker than the black cowl he wears. He shuns all company, humans and leprechauns. He distrusts all outsiders. He treats this land like his private property. If he smells a whiff of trouble, he'll act first and never bother t' ask questions. Ye be strangers and he won't take kindly t' yer presence. Be careful."

"We will," the Baron replied. "The fire explains Bonehand's name, but not why he would steal the Flute; especially if he's your friend."

"The Flute brings joy t' the animals called by it," Ian replied. "But it also put 'em under the control of whoever's playin'. They become like innocent children who do whatever they're asked, even if it's bad fer 'em. I told me friend about the Flute—even showed him its power once. He got real upset. Said it shouldn't be used t' control free creatures, even if it did make 'em happy. He wanted me t' get rid of it so it wouldn't fall into the wrong hands. But I said I couldn't just throw away somethin' I'd been charged t' protect. We argued about it a lot."

Matterhorn scratched the hair behind his left ear as he listened. There were valuable clues in these details that needed ferreting out.

"I was away at the time of the fire," Ian continued. "When I got back and heard of the tragedy, I tried t' console me friend. He wouldn't have it. Blamed the whole mess on me, he did. Said the soldiers had come lookin' fer the Flute and that more would follow. I didn't see him again till the day before me Flute disappeared. He refused t' share me fire, but he saw where I was camped. I think he came later that night and took the Flute. I doubt the instrument can be destroyed. Still, if Bonehand has enough time, he'll hide the Flute where it'll never be found."

The king's eyes grew moist. "Do what ye can. And if it's gold ye be wantin' in return I've a pot or two I can spare."

"That won't be necessary," the Baron said.

Ian gave a shudder of relief. Then he pulled himself to his full height, raised his right hand toward the Travelers and gave them his blessing. "May the sun warm yer face, the wind cool yer back, and the Maker guide yer way." With that, he walked into the forest.

Questions in the Dark

BACK at camp, Matterhorn wrote down what the Baron had said about truth as the author of that clever phrase rinsed their dishes. The moon was so bright and the stars so numerous that he didn't need the firelight. But he was still in the dark about why the Sword had selected *him* and sent him to Ireland via First Realm. He was smart, but no genius. He was a good athlete, but years away from his full potential. He liked adventure, but hadn't had much in his young life. Surely there were thousands of adults better suited to finding the missing Flute.

The fire crackled and spat a chunk of smoldering ash into Matterhorn's lap. He swatted at the orange ember while Aaron laughed and splashed him with water.

"What did you think of Ian?" the Baron asked.

Matterhorn put away his quote book and said, "I thought leprechauns were fairy-like creatures. Ian was taller, and, well, more earthy, than I would have expected."

"You mean he was dirty and smelled funny. That's the difference between books and real life."

"Did Queen Bea tell you why the Flute was given to the leprechauns?" Matterhorn wondered. "If the Talis was made for First Realm, what's it doing here?"

The Baron dried his hands and propped himself against a tree. "She didn't tell me much about Ian," he replied, "just that his family had been entrusted with the Flute and that it had been stolen. Several of the Ten Talis have recently been hidden on Earth because of the trouble brewing in the Realm."

"Recently?" Matterhorn repeated. "Ian's story made it sound like it's been in his family for generations."

"And that's true, from an earthly perspective," the Baron said. "But First Realm's timeline is different from ours."

"Do you know what sort of problems they're having?" was Matterhorn's next question.

Aaron shrugged. He did know, yet wasn't sure how much to burden Matterhorn with on his first night. "The Queen's been pretty tight-lipped about it all. You'd better ask Her Majesty next time you see her."

"When will that be?"

"That depends on how long it takes us to find the Flute." The Baron got up and untied the bedroll from the bottom of his pack. He kicked a pile of leaves into a makeshift mattress and made his bed.

Matterhorn did likewise. The bedroll on his pack had a foil lining that reminded him of the space blanket his dad kept in the car for emergencies. This was the first time he'd thought of his family since this adventure began. His parents must be worried sick. His sister would have walked home alone from school. Victor would be there by now. They would all be upset by his disappearance. Dad would call the police. They would search the library and find the book at his carrel. But would they be able to follow him through the portal?

Seeing the book in his mind's eye sent a chill through his body. Slowly he spoke the title aloud. *"The Sword and the Flute."*

"What did you say?" Aaron asked.

"The Sword and the Flute. That's the name of the book I got sucked into. I know what it means now." But he didn't know how the volume had found its way onto Mr. Rickets' shelves. Questions piled up in his brain until he reached mental gridlock. He quit thinking about them and hoped everything would make more sense in the morning. Lying on his back with his arms crossed over his chest, Matterhorn searched the indigo sky until he spotted some familiar constellations.

Sleeping under the stars was not a new or frightening experience. The Horns spent their summers camping across America. Matterhorn's dad was a freelance writer and could set his own schedule. His mom taught psychology at the community college and refused to teach during summer term.

Matterhorn had been as low as Death Valley and as high as Pikes Peak. He'd been fossil hunting in the

Badlands, bird watching in the Everglades, salmon fishing in the Pacific Northwest, and backpacking along the Appalachian Trail. He'd gone swimming in both oceans and several lakes in between. His favorite was Echo Lake in Montana. He had traveled to a lot of places in his short life and he could now add Ireland to the list—except no one would believe him.

His thoughts returned home. The district championship match would be over by now. Who had started in goal in his place? Not Rusby. But there wasn't anyone else to fill in . . . they would have lost for sure. He wondered how the coach and the other kids felt about his disappearance. Had he been declared a missing person yet?

Matterhorn played with his ponytail as he mused. He liked the look and feel of it and thought about letting his hair grow when he got home. Since he would no doubt revert to his twelve-year-old self, he would have to start from scratch.

The prospect startled him. If his body returned to adolescence, what about his mind? Would he remember any of this: Queen Bea, First Realm, the Sword of Truth, Aaron the Baron? What about Ireland, Broc, and Ian?

Maybe his memory would be erased so he couldn't reveal the activities of Travelers or the existence of First Realm.

A still more frightening possibility suddenly occurred to him.

What if he never made it home?

Time Talk

MATTERHORN awoke dazed and confused. The first thing he saw was a straggle of red chest hair sticking out from under a folded pair of brawny arms. *What in the—*. Then he remembered that he had been super-sized. He felt the stubble on his chin with hands that looked too big to be his. But they responded to commands from his brain, so they had to belong to him.

His appetite had also grown and he hoped breakfast would be better than supper.

The horses returned while the Baron and Matterhorn were erasing all evidence of their campsite. Matterhorn walked over to Broc, patted his neck and rubbed the peculiar birthmark. But the animal remained stiff until Matterhorn produced a candy bar.

"What a break!" Aaron exclaimed, approaching his own mount. "Yesterday they came to take us to Ian. I didn't expect them to show up today. But I never turn down a free ride."

"Do you think they know where we need to go?" Matterhorn asked, wiping the horse slobber off his palm and onto his pants.

"Only one way to find out." They loaded up their packs and climbed aboard, where they sat for a pair of minutes while nothing happened. "I guess we're driving today," the Baron said at last.

Heading their mounts north from the spring, they eventually ran into a large stream, which they crossed and followed west.

Echo Lake moved to the number two spot on Matterhorn's list that afternoon when he and Aaron topped a piney ridge and discovered the valley of the lake. From their vantage point it looked like an immense earthen funnel filled with melted glass. The transparent edges sparkled with sunlight and its center plunged to sapphire depths.

Matterhorn was glad to dismount. His back and rear were sore from a second day on horseback. The insides of his legs felt raw and his knees throbbed. Broc looked as fresh as he had that morning, despite having hauled a heavy passenger up and down the hilly terrain.

"You could at least have the decency to sweat," Matterhorn complained as he rubbed Broc's neck. The horse tossed his mane and went off in search of tender shoots for supper. Matterhorn opted for a soak in the crisp, clear water to soothe his aching muscles. Swarms of dragonflies played tag among the marsh marigolds and water lilies where he floated.

The Baron, meanwhile, found a few fallen trees and decided to make a raft. Using his survival saw—a cutting band between two rings—he trimmed the limbs off three logs and lashed them together. He had Matterhorn scratch in the mud for worms while he rigged the tackle. Then they made for deep water and began fishing with lines tied to their fingers.

This secluded lake seldom had visitors, so the native stock grew to unusual size. Matterhorn saw an enormous old-timer drift into their shadow. It was by far the biggest fish he'd ever seen in the wild, measuring seven feet from nose to tail.

The hungry sturgeon took Matterhorn's bait on the way by, dragging him off the raft. Matterhorn grabbed for the line to keep from losing his finger. The Baron jumped in and thrashed around with his knife until he cut the monster loose.

As they clung to the raft, the Baron's laugh rolled across the valley. "I didn't realize fishing here would be so dangerous."

"I'm glad that one got away," Matterhorn gasped. He bit the loop from his finger and soaked the sore digit in the water.

That evening they pitched camp high on the eastern slope in the last swatch of daylight. They ate dried food and watched the steady stream of animals coming to drink: sika deer, red foxes, skittish rabbits. At one point, Matterhorn glimpsed a small white horse cresting the ridge across the way, but the animal disappeared before he could get a second look. Had there been a horn on the creature's head?

Matterhorn's aches and pains made it hard to sleep. Rolling onto his stomach, he propped his chin on his hands and stared at Aaron, resting a few feet away. "Are you asleep?" he asked.

"I'm working on it," came a faint reply.

"Can you answer a question first?"

"Fire away."

"How did we travel back in time?"

The Baron sighed and leaned up on an elbow. This was going to take a while. "Picture the multiverse like a balloon being blown up by the Maker." He did a mime of inflating a balloon. "Time-space is like the skin on the balloon. Saying "when" something happened, such as your birthday or the first moon landing, is just pointing out the place on the balloon where that event occurred.

"When we came here," the Baron patted the ground, "we traveled to a specific address in time-space. Since it happens to be farther down the balloon than where you live, you think of it as in the past, but that depends on your point of view. Ever hear of superstring theory?"

Matterhorn nodded, remembering the time Uncle Al had tried to explain it to him. He knew it had something to do with gravity, yet most of the details had flown over his head and out the window.

"Current superstring theory, also known as M theory, says there are at least eleven dimensions," the Baron explained. "Actually there are more. Most of these extra dimensions are quantum-sized, meaning they're incredibly tiny. But if you know how to uncurl them, you can move around time-space on your own miniature subway system."

"If time travel is possible," Matterhorn protested, "why haven't I read about it?"

"You have. Only you didn't realize it because there are all kinds of ways to get into portals. You can be sucked into one like Dorothy in *The Wizard of Oz*. Or fall into one as Alice did in Wonderland. Or accidentally walk into one like Peter and Susan and Edmund and Lucy did in *The Chronicles of Narnia*. Portals adapt to the time in which they open."

"But those are just stories," Matterhorn protested.

"The best fiction is often based on fact," the Baron countered. "Sometimes it's hard to tell the difference."

Indeed, the book Matterhorn had been reading only yesterday—*A Connecticut Yankee in King Arthur's Court*—underscored the Baron's point. The recollection brought another question to mind. "The Hall of Portals where we met," he asked, "was that in the past or the future?"

"Neither and both."

"Now you're really confusing me."

"Well, then, let me throw more light on the subject."

The Baron got up to put another branch on the fire. The next second, a heavy object fell from the sky and stuck in the ground where his head had been.

UFO

THE UFO—unidentified falling object—looked like a large bone. It was stark white and thick as a man's forearm. Its sharpened point had been driven into the soft ground by its speed and mass.

"Someone must have a bone to pick with us," the Baron said, glancing over at the still-quivering stake.

Matterhorn wasn't as calm. He had almost done something he hadn't done in years—wet his bed. He sat up and said in a shaky voice, "Wh-where did that come from?"

Staring into the night, the Baron replied, "I'm not sure how it got here, but I'll give you three guesses who sent it, and the first two don't count."

The surrounding dark became more threatening than it had been a minute before. "What do we do now?" Matterhorn bleated.

"Let's scoot under those trees to protect ourselves from any more bone bombs," Aaron said. He pulled his bedroll near the base of a large Douglas fir. Matterhorn did likewise.

54

"As for a ground attack . . ." The Baron drew from his pack what appeared to be three metal toothbrushes. Tiny red buds stuck out where the bristles should have been. From Matterhorn's pack he removed three disks the size of hockey pucks that had been attached to the lining. He put a brush in each puck and placed them in a triangle around the camp.

When the Baron finished and crawled beneath the tree, Matterhorn asked, "Are those some kind of motion detectors?"

"They're electric eyes."

"Like the ones that open automatic doors?"

"Not quite. The ion-battery bases generate an electric current that flows between the poles. Anyone crossing the beam is in for quite a shock."

"From those tiny things?" Matterhorn said skeptically.

The Baron pointed to their packs. "See those metallic strips on the top and sides? Those are accelerated solar collectors. They've been charging the batteries since we arrived. Each one contains a day's worth of sunlight, more than enough to disable any prowlers. By the way," he added, snuggling down into his bedding, "be careful if you get up before me. I don't like the smell of burnt skin."

Matterhorn felt slightly safer as he lay down on the fragrant boughs.

The next thing he knew the sun was poking him in the face. He sat up and rubbed the sleep from his eyes. A thin layer of dew glazed the buttercup and clover countryside.

The fear he felt the night before didn't survive the dawn. He heard Aaron snoring softly a few feet away.

When he glanced over at his partner, he realized their security system had a flaw. Anything on two—or four—legs would have had trouble sneaking into camp. But a creature with no legs, such as the one curled up on the Baron's chest, had no problem paying them a visit.

"Aaron," Matterhorn whispered urgently. "Aaron."

The Baron stirred and opened his eyes. When his new hood ornament came into focus, he stiffened like a corpse. Except for his eyes, which quickly outgrew their sockets. Not many things frightened him, but one of them sat coiled twelve inches from his nose.

Matterhorn knew there was good reason to be scared. Having recently done a science project on poisonous snakes, he recognized the zigzag black markings of a European viper. He also knew there weren't supposed to be any snakes in Ireland. According to legend, Saint Patrick had driven them all away in the fifth century.

He liked snakes, even poisonous ones. You just had to be careful around them, that's all. He would have had a pet snake if his sister weren't deathly afraid of them. Without knowing where the idea came from, he knew what to do. Taking the Sword hilt quietly from his belt, he willed the blade to extend. Slowly he laid it between the serpent's head and the Baron's. Then he slid it carefully under the snake, whose tongue began flicking in and out.

The Baron's eyes got wider by the flick.

At this point, Matterhorn raised the temperature of the Sword with his mind. He wasn't sure how he knew he could do this; he just did. He felt the warmth in contrast to the morning chill. So did the viper, and it stretched full-length along the blade until its head almost touched Matterhorn's hand.

What an elegant creature, Matterhorn thought. He saw intelligence in those reptilian eyes. He wished his slinky friend well as he lifted the blade and put it on the ground on his other side. Then he willed the shaft to cool. The snake disliked the change and slithered off into the bushes.

Aaron's bedroll, which had been rigid as a bar of silver, deflated as its occupant exhaled. "Whew. I owe you one."

"In that case," Matterhorn replied as he laid back and clasped his hands behind his head, "I'll have breakfast in bed. Anything except burnt cheese sandwiches."

After serving powdered eggs on toast, the Baron took the security system apart while Matterhorn studied the bone that had almost orphaned him in Ireland. He scrutinized it for clues, wishing he had the powerful microscope from his chemistry set at home. Yet even with his naked eye, Matterhorn learned a lot in a few minutes.

"This thing is fossilized," he said when the Baron wandered over. "That explains why it's so heavy. It must be from a large animal that got caught in a bog and got petrified. What's interesting is how the end was sharpened. Run your finger along this edge."

"It feels smooth."

"And that tells us—"

"That the point was made by a grinding wheel," the Baron said, "not a sword or axe."

"Elementary, my dear Watson!" Matterhorn cried. "And these gray streaks?"

"Friction burns," the Baron replied. "And don't call me dear."

Matterhorn got to his feet. "Since electricity hasn't been harnessed yet, the grinding wheel must be water driven. That would require a stream moving fast enough to turn a mill wheel. Like the one we crossed our first day here."

"Then that's the place to pick up the trail," the Baron concluded. "Thank you Mr. Bonehand!" he shouted skyward. "You have given us our first clue."

Hit and Run

Chapter 12

T HEY backtracked to the stream they had followed
earlier and traced it west. Matterhorn daydreamed
while they trotted along its green-carpeted banks. The
gurgling river and Broc's gentle gait rocked him to the
brink of sleep.

The Baron, on the other horse, sat wide awake, strain-
ing to get a fix on whoever had been trailing them all
morning. The tracker was good, but he'd made one or two
tiny mistakes—a twig snap here, a careless footfall there—
enough for the Baron to guess his presence. In the past, he
would have been as clueless as Matterhorn about their
unseen tail. But not now, not since his adventure with the
greatest tracker of all. The Queen had told him some fan-
tastic stories about this other Traveler, an Aboriginal
known as Nate the Great. After one trip with him, the
Baron realized the Queen had been somewhat mistaken.

The man was even better than the myth.

Nate the Great had tracked every kind of animal, yet
he never killed for sport. Built like a log with legs, he

could still fold himself into the tiniest hiding places. He could walk on snow without leaving tracks. He could smell bacon cooking a mile away and tell you which side of the pig it came from. The only way you knew Nate was around was if he walked up and shook your hand. Otherwise, forget it.

Nate had shown Aaron how to check suspicious sounds on the trail by varying his pace. Twice that morning the Baron had let Matterhorn and Broc get a few yards ahead and then halted. Both times he heard telltale noises.

When the sun reached high noon, the Baron decided to do some tracking of his own. "Let's give the animals a rest," he said in a loud voice.

They parked their mounts beside a natural windbreak of poplars. Matterhorn knelt on moss as soft as mouse fur and stuck his face in the river for a long drink. The Baron leaned his pack against a tree and squatted on a rock. Cupping the refreshing water to his lips, he said between sips, "You shouldn't drink that way; it leaves you vulnerable."

"Vulnerable to what?" Matterhorn asked, wiping his chin on his sleeve.

"To an attack from behind. We're being followed. Don't turn around."

Matterhorn stared straight ahead and lowered his voice. "We are? By whom?"

"That's what I intend to find out," the Baron said. "Wait here. And whatever you do, don't leave. The last thing we need is to get separated." With a wink and a smile he slipped between the poplars and vanished.

He wiggled stealthily through a tangle of underbrush until he came to a game trail hedged by waist-high ferns. When the path widened into a clearing, he skirted the fringe to stay hidden. Off to the right he heard a whooshing noise and spun in time to see a rope tied to three rocks coming in low and fast. The weapon wrapped around his legs, tripping him forward.

Before he could get to his knees, a hood came down over his head. It was tied off so that he could barely breathe, much less scream for help. Strong hands jerked his arms back and bound his wrists. His ankles got the same treatment. Then he was flipped onto a litter tied to the south end of a northbound animal, which began picking its way through the trees, dragging its heavy wooden tail.

The whole episode took less than a minute.

As the Baron lay on the litter, stunned but unhurt, he tried to piece together what had just happened. He couldn't see anything, but he kept his ears open for clues. It was no use; his captors were quiet as poachers. They didn't want him dead, the Baron reasoned, or else he would be. They hadn't searched him for valuables either. That meant kidnapping must be their aim.

But who were "they"?

The pace of the pack animal convinced the Baron he was attached to a donkey, not a horse. The stretcher turned out to be several inches shorter than its passenger, so he had to bend his knees upward to prevent the ground from pulling off his boots. To keep his muscles from cramping he did isometric exercises and abdominal crunches.

He couldn't move his arms, but his fingers could just reach his belt. As time passed he was able to work it around his body until he touched the slim buckle. He pressed the silver stud holding it to the leather. This activated the receiver in his backpack. The homing device had an eight-mile radius. He hoped Matterhorn would figure out what the beeping meant before the donkey clopped out of range.

A razor blade lay hidden along the bottom edge of the belt. If his kidnappers shifted him around when they stopped for the night, he might be able to cut his ropes and escape. The tracking stud and cutting blade were only two of the many tools on the Baron. He also wore a thin nylon pouch around his stomach that held several useful items including the fixings for a powerful bomb. The detonators were stored in the hollow heel of his left boot. The heel of his right boot contained a mini survival kit of fishing line and hooks, a miniature magnifying glass for starting fires and some penicillin capsules in case of infection.

"Be prepared for everything," his mother always said, "and you'll be prepared for anything." As the only child of a single parent, the Baron was very close to his mom. His father had abandoned them years ago. His mom worked two jobs and did her best to be both parents. By her simple words and daily example, she taught Aaron to be resourceful and to never give up.

Although his situation was desperate, the Baron refused to believe he would die in Ireland. He had learned in his travels that all things, including the unexpected and the painful, worked together for good when one served the Maker.

He hoped that applied to being kidnapped.

The afternoon plodded along as slowly as the donkey. Aaron tried to keep a cool head, but it was impossible inside the black hood, which smelled like dirty socks. Sticky sweat crawled over his face and oozed down his neck. The wetness made him realize how parched he was. If only he'd taken a bigger drink at the stream.

Hours later, the one-donkey parade finally stopped. The Baron was dumped on the hard ground. He rolled over and stretched. To his left he heard the snapping of branches, followed by the crackling of a fire. Next came the sizzle of frying meat. Rabbit, by the smell of it. The bag loosened around his neck and a callused hand with dirty fingernails shoved a slice of something greasy into his mouth. He chewed greedily and was thankful for the squirt of water he got before the bag cinched closed for the night.

In a few hours he would try to escape. For now he would make himself comfortable and get some sleep. He wondered if Matterhorn had figured out the homing signal. If so, what would he do about it?

The Baron would soon find out. And his kidnappers would soon learn that they had made not one, but two strategic mistakes that day.

The first was grabbing the Baron.

The second was not grabbing Matterhorn.

Search and Rescue

WHILE the Baron was being bagged, tagged, and dragged away, Matterhorn sat waiting by the stream.

And waiting.

And waiting.

Ten minutes passed.

Then twenty.

Matterhorn fretted about the Baron. He leaned against a soft rock and considered the possibilities. Maybe Aaron couldn't find anyone because no one was out there. Maybe he'd gotten lost. The Baron wasn't in trouble, Matterhorn reassured himself, or he would have yelled for help.

Matterhorn sat very still and listened hard for unusual noises.

All was quiet. Too quiet.

The next thing he knew, he felt a wet nose nuzzling him awake and looked up to see Broc standing over him.

He'd fallen asleep!

A wave of hot panic lifted him to his feet. How could he have dozed off? How long had he been asleep? How long had the Baron been gone?

He felt ashamed at his laziness. Regardless of the Baron's command to stay put, he had to do something. And he wasn't the only one in turmoil. The Baron's horse nickered and fidgeted from foot to foot to foot to foot. Did he know his rider wasn't coming back?

"You can leave if you want," Matterhorn said to the animal.

The stallion nodded and took off.

Matterhorn shifted his gaze to Broc, who stood still as a stone horse in a park. Only his ears moved, tilting forward.

"Do you want to go, too?"

The horse shook his head and gave an angry snort.

Relieved, Matterhorn asked, "What do we do now, Broc?"

Just a few days earlier, Matterhorn had been minding his own business in the library at school. Now he was lost and alone in medieval Ireland. Someone tried to kill his partner last night. Had they succeeded today?

While the situation around Matterhorn unraveled, the clouds above him knit themselves into a wooly gray blanket. The unfamiliar landscape grew somber and the scent of rain seeped through the sultry afternoon. Thunderclouds gathered on the horizon and flung lightning bolts at each other.

Matterhorn's mood should have been as gloomy as the weather. Instead, he chose to get excited. The courage of the called and committed surged through him. The peril was overwhelming for a twelve-year-old boy, but he no longer thought of himself as a kid. The Sword of Truth had called him to be a knight—that's what the Queen had told him. And the Sword couldn't lie; he was ready to believe that. It would guide and protect him as he searched for the Baron; he was ready to believe that, too.

Now, if he only knew what to do! Being a novice in the hero business, he wondered how to proceed. His mind raced. His heart pounded.

Boom! Boom! Boom!

Beep! Beep! Beep!

Boom! Boom! Beep! Beep!

Wait a minute. Did hearts beep?

The noise was coming from the Baron's pack. Matterhorn fished out a slim metal box with a radar-like screen. A dim green light flashed near its edge in time with the beeps.

Probably a homing device, Matterhorn guessed, as he saw the words "HOMING DEVICE" stenciled under the screen. The Baron must have activated a tracking signal, which meant he was still alive!

Matterhorn had to move fast, and he now had two packs to carry. Did he have the right to involve Broc in a risky rescue?

Broc began snorting, nodding, and pawing the ground, making it clear he wasn't about to be left behind.

"Are you with me?" Matterhorn asked.

Another fierce flurry of nods.

"Then let's go."

The kidnappers hadn't bothered to hide their trail. Matterhorn didn't need the Baron's beeper and switched it off. Broc steamed down the parallel tracks left by the litter. Horse and rider rushed past massive oaks whose intertwined arms shielded them from most of the rain. Hanging ivy, tree ferns, and wild strawberry plants formed the sides of the verdant tunnel through which they churned.

They caught up to the kidnappers by nightfall. From a safe distance, Matterhorn surveyed the sprawling meadow where they had stopped. He watched the six short men pitch camp. These were dwarfs—twice as tall as leprechauns and twice as thick. Their heads were screwed tight to their broad shoulders. They had full mustaches and bushy beards grown down to their barrel chests. Their powerful limbs made them look like a troop of miniature Turkish weightlifters.

Three of the six wore red kerchiefs. All had flat metal chains on the outside of their rough cotton shirts and deerskin vests. Black leather boots matched their wide leather belts, which sported ornate iron buckles. The belts also held an assortment of short-handled axes and knives.

These were *not* Snow White's dwarfs.

Matterhorn spied the Baron near the fire, hooded like a cat about to be drowned. He was in no shape to help with his rescue. Matterhorn would be on his own. He had the cover of darkness, the element of surprise, and the Sword of Truth. Now all he needed was a plan.

He spoke quietly to Broc. The more time they spent together, the more he realized this was one smart horse. "What do you think, Broc? Option A: we can leave the

Baron where he is and follow the group. Perhaps they'll lead us to Bonehand and the Flute."

Broc tossed his head from side to side.

"How about Option B?" Matterhorn said. "You create a diversion to draw some dwarfs away while I overpower the rest and free the Baron." He was twice their size; maybe he could handle two or three.

Another flurry of no-nods. Broc tilted his head to the right and looked down his long nose as if to imply, "Is that the best you can do?"

Matterhorn reddened at the visual rebuke. "Okay," he blurted. "Option C: I wait till everyone's asleep, sneak in, cut the Baron loose, and we run for it. I doubt the dwarfs will post a guard. They didn't bother to cover their tracks, so they're not expecting to be followed. Maybe they thought I'd hightail it for home." Like I know how to get there, Matterhorn thought.

He agonized over these possibilities for a minute until Broc chose Option D. He put his muzzle in the middle of Matterhorn's back and shoved him toward the fire.

Twelve steely eyes focused on Matterhorn as he stumbled into view. In his panic, he recalled a quote from Aesop he'd written in his quote book not long ago: "It is easy to be brave from a safe distance." Now he had to be brave up close.

He scritched the Sword of Truth from his belt and said as gruffly as he could, "You guys are in a lot of trouble."

Teamwork

IF this show of boldness was supposed to intimidate the kidnappers, it failed completely. At six to one, they liked their odds against this tall redhead. Even if he did have a mean-looking sword, he would never get close enough to use it. The nearest dwarf noted the flush of fear on Matterhorn's face and the way his hands trembled. With a sneer he plugged one nostril with his thumb and blew out the contents of the other in Matterhorn's direction. Then he reached for the rock-and-rope weapon he'd used on the Baron and hurled it in one smooth motion.

The Sword sliced downward on its own, cutting the rope like dental floss. The stones flew by on either side. Matterhorn was amazed that he'd managed to hang on to the hilt.

Another dwarf yanked a short axe from his belt and charged. No sooner did he have the weapon raised than Matterhorn lunged—or was pulled—forward. He turned the axe into a stick by chopping off its metal head. A lightning backswing reduced the stick to a stub. Holding the tip of the now-glowing blade an inch from the attacker's chest, Matterhorn heard himself bark, "Sit!"

The stunned man dropped so fast his beard flew up into his face.

All this commotion scared the donkey that had been loosely tied to a sapling. The frightened beast jerked free and raced across the clearing. Matterhorn dodged the runaway, which gave another dwarf the chance to slink up behind and grab him, pinning his arms to his sides and making him drop the Sword.

Though a bit awkward with weapons, Matterhorn understood wrestling. Instinctively he responded to this bear hug by stepping forward on his outside foot, lowering his center of gravity and dipping his left shoulder. When the dwarf shifted to maintain his hold, Matterhorn back-stepped and jerked an arm free. But when he spun to throw a headlock, his elbow sailed over his stocky opponent's head.

The dwarf tightened his grip and arched his back. Matterhorn was about to be pile-driven face first into the dirt when a rock zinged in and clocked the dwarf. His face went slack, so did his grip, and he slid down the back of Matterhorn's legs.

Forty feet away, Aaron the Baron picked up another stone with his left hand. While his captors had been focusing on Matterhorn, he'd cut his ropes on the belt blade and removed the hood. He had no trouble hitting his target with the baseball-sized rock. After all, he had hurled hundreds of strikes from a pitcher's mound, and he knew how to dust a batter who hugged the plate. This guy had definitely been hugging.

Now the odds weren't so good and the remaining dwarfs bolted for the forest. Another beaner from the Baron dropped the slowest runner before he reached the trees. The others disappeared, but not for long. They came shooting back into the clearing, stubby legs pumping, a few feet ahead of Broc's thundering hooves. The horse snorted in triumph as he corralled the fugitives.

"Good job, Broc!" Matterhorn cried. The shout tightened a ring of pain around his chest. He must have a couple of bruised ribs. He gingerly picked up his Sword and walked over to the Baron. "Are you okay?"

"I'm stiff," the Baron replied, rubbing the blood back into his wrists, "but I'll be fine. You did a brave thing taking on those dwarfs. Thanks for coming after me."

Matterhorn blushed at the compliment.

Ten minutes later they had a six-pack of sullen dwarfs tied with their own ropes and stewing in their own juices. The rancid sweat was so overpowering that Matterhorn and the Baron moved to a breathable distance and plopped down to rest.

"So you're a southpaw," Matterhorn said. "Where'd you learn to throw like that?"

"Little League."

"How long ago did you play baseball?" Matterhorn asked in surprise.

"Last month I pitched a one-hitter in the city play-offs." The Baron grinned. "I don't travel *all* the time you know."

It suddenly dawned on Matterhorn that Aaron's story might be similar to his own.

"How old are you in the real world?"

"All worlds are real," the Baron said. "Back home I'm thirteen."

"You're just a year older than me," Matterhorn said. "How long have you been traveling? Where are you from? Do your parents know you're in Ireland? Do they worry about you when you're gone? Do you—"

The Baron raised a hand. "Slow down, slow down. I've been traveling since I was nine. I'm from the good ol' U.S. of A. My parents don't worry about me. At least my dad doesn't. He left when I was three. My mom doesn't know I travel."

"How can that be?" Matterhorn interrupted.

"You'll see when you get back. Now, are you going to keep grilling me or can we ask my kidnappers a few questions?"

They approached the dwarfs. The Baron stood, hands on hips, and scanned the six stony faces. "Who wants to explain what you were up to? Am I so ugly that you felt the need to stick a bag on my head and drag me away from civilization?"

"You're not *that* ugly," Matterhorn said.

The captors-turned-captives remained mute.

"If you won't talk," Matterhorn said, breaking the long silence, "I'll have to read your minds."

Six jaws tightened in unison.

"You don't think I can do it?" Matterhorn asked. "You're a tough crowd. However, with the help of my faithful assistant, Aaron the Baron, I will mystify one and all."

"Ready when you are, Sir Matterhorn," the Baron said. He had absolutely no idea what was going on.

"Very well," Matterhorn said. "I will now select my first victim, er, subject." He moved in front of the second dwarf from the left. This was the one the Baron had beaned. He had a nasty purple bruise spreading from his right temple down his cheek. He might be more likely to talk.

"Anything you want to say before we begin?"

The stark silence matched the dwarf's hard stare.

"Since our volunteer has lost his voice, I will read his thoughts using my mind—and my Sword," Matterhorn announced. He laid the blade in the startled man's lap and placed his hands on the dwarf's head.

Matterhorn had pieced together an idea, but he wasn't sure it would work. He recalled the shock the Sword had given him in the Hall of Portals when he had lied. He also remembered how he commanded the blade to heat up when he saved the Baron from the snake. If he could just combine those two experiences . . .

"Ask him his name, Baron, and I'll answer for him," Matterhorn said.

"What's your name?" the Baron said, a slow grin sliding across his face. Now he got it.

A moment later so did the unfortunate dwarf when Matterhorn answered in a loud voice, "My name is Amos!"

The jolt knocked the little man over, straightening his frizzy beard and curling his eyelashes at the same time.

Matterhorn sat the dazed dwarf upright as if reset-ting a bowling pin. He winced at the pain in his ribs and stifled a yelp. Putting the Sword in place, he rested his hands like before. "Guess I'm a bit rusty," he said. "Shall we try again?"

The dwarf sucked in his upper lip, bit his mustache, and said nothing.

"What's your name?" the Baron asked again.

"Bob," Matterhorn said, willing the Sword to shock once more.

Zap!

Over toppled the dwarf.

Reset.

Matterhorn held the blade above the man's quivering knees and stared into his watery eyes. "This is the Sword of Truth," Matterhorn said. "You can tell me your name—or I can guess my way through the alphabet."

The dwarf fainted.

"His name's Zeke," said the dwarf sitting next in line. "And before you use that thing on me, the name's Diller. What else you wanna know?"

Clean Shave

THE dwarf who spoke up was the one who had used the throwing rocks on the Baron and had tried to use them on Matterhorn.

"Who's in charge of this band of brigands?" Matterhorn asked.

"I am," Diller said in a baritone voice. A missing front tooth gave him a slight lisp. "But we ain't brigands. We're smithies by trade."

"Kidnapping is strange work for blacksmiths," the Baron said.

"We wouldn't have taken the job, only we was desperate. Few travelers come this way since the fire. Work's been hard to find."

"Who hired you?"

"Don't know," Diller replied. "Karn told us a man was lookin' for some muscle to get rid of a couple of nosy strangers. Promised us a bag of gold if we made you disappear."

"Who's Karn?" the Baron pressed.

"He's the lep what runs the tradin' post where we get
our supplies."

"Lep?"

"You know, leprechaun," Diller said.

"Where were you taking me?"

"To an island off the coast."

"Then what?"

"Then we was gonna let you go. Honest. Karn just
told us to get rid of you. He didn't say we had to kill you.
That ain't our way. So we decided to grab one of you—
didn't matter which one—and take you to this island we
know.

"We left a trail what the other fella could follow," he
explained. "We didn't expect you to be so quick about
it." He glared at Matterhorn. "Once we stranded one of
you, we thought it'd take the other guy a while to rescue
his friend. That would give us time to collect our gold."

"Sorry to spoil your plans," Matterhorn said, "but
we have plans of our own." He tossed some wood on the
fire and said to Broc, "Keep an eye on this bunch while
the Baron and I take a walk."

The horse reared and stomped the ground near the
dwarf's bound feet. They scrunched closer together and
tried to pull their legs into their chests.

"These guys are a few pepperonis short of a good
pizza," Matterhorn said when they got out of earshot.
"What shall we do with them?"

"We'll have to let them go," Aaron said.

"How can we keep them from following us and caus-
ing more trouble?"

"Leave that to me. But first, let's see what else we can learn."

Back at the fire, Aaron sat on his heels in front of Diller. "Tell us what we want to know and we'll cut you loose," he promised.

"But we don't know nothin'," Diller started to protest.

"I'm not talking about who hired you. I want to know if there's a mill around here."

Puzzled, Diller said, "It's about ten miles downriver from where we snatched you."

"How about this Karn fellow? Where's his trading post?"

"Right next to the mill," Diller said. "It's not far from the main road. That all you wanna know?"

"No," Aaron answered. "Have you ever heard of Ian's Flute?"

Diller cleared his throat. "We heard of it, sure."

"Did you know it's been stolen?"

"Heard that, too, and that the leps been goin' crazy lookin' for it."

"Any idea who took it?"

"Nope."

Matterhorn stepped forward with the Sword of Truth, but the dwarf didn't flinch.

"Use that if you want," Diller said, "but I'm tellin' the truth."

Matterhorn believed him.

"One more question," the Baron said, getting to his feet. "Does the name 'Bonehand' mean anything to you?"

A sudden shudder rippled through the group. "That man's gone evil," said the dwarf on the far right. "Dresses all in black and slinks around like a ghost. Don't talk no more, just watches everythin'. People say he caught the soldiers what started the fire that ruin't his hand. None of them's ever been found."

"That fire turned his heart coal black and diamond hard," piped in another dwarf. "He ain't a man to mess with."

"Did you ever stop to think he might be the one you're working for?" the Baron asked.

The dwarfs looked stunned. "If this is Bonehand's business," Diller said slowly, "then we're even sorrier we got involved."

"You'll be sorrier still if you follow us," the Baron said. "Give us your word that you won't bother us again."

After the dwarfs followed their leader in making the promise, the Baron cut their ropes and handed Diller back his knife. He took it with stumpy fingers that ended in the black crescents of dirty fingernails. The lines on his calloused palms looked like they'd been tattooed there with black ink.

"Now use it to shave your beard," the Baron ordered.

Diller looked as though the big man had slapped him. "Do what?" he bellowed.

"You heard me. All of you will shave—or else."

"Or else what?" Diller shot back.

Matterhorn drew his Sword and Broc stamped the ground.

"Or else we'll tie you to the trees and let the animals see to you. Or maybe Bonehand will come by to check on his flunkies."

"I can't show my naked face back home," Diller moaned. "I'd die of shame. I've had my whiskers since I was fourteen."

The Baron shrugged. "Then I guess you'll have to stay in the woods till they grow back. It shouldn't take long for hairy guys like you to get presentable."

The dwarfs fussed and fumed, but in the end they each took the knife and did the deed. The look in Broc's eyes and the otherworldly light in the Sword made it unavoidable. Afterwards, they gathered their shorn locks and fed them to the flames. The terrible stink was a fitting expression of their grief.

They didn't stay sad for long, though. Their shame was soon lightened with laughter at the discovery that Diller and another dwarf named Peat had deep clefts in their chins.

"Where'd you get that crease?" howled Zeke, who had recovered from his shock treatment. "Your chin looks like a baby's butt!"

"Feels like one too," Diller replied as he scratched his tender jaw. "But at least I ain't as pig-ugly as the rest of you."

The youngest of them, a fellow called Red Flint because of his ruddy features and sharp nose, decided to shave his whole head.

"Young 'uns," Diller said disapprovingly.

Matterhorn returned the dwarfs' other weapons so they could hunt for food while waiting for their beards to grow back. Touched by the gesture, Diller said, "You're honorable men. I'm glad you came by no harm."

It was well after midnight when Matterhorn, the Baron, and Broc began retracing the drag marks to where this whole misadventure had begun. High overhead a stealthy bird watched them go. Even at night its beady eyes could see the fleas on a rat's back from a half mile up.

Another set of eyes followed them at ground level. This tracker was much more skilled than the dwarfs, and more than content to stay in the shadows.

For now.

Karn the Lep

THE weary Travelers made it back to the stream by dawn and caught a few Zs before going in search of Karn. They had little trouble with the dwarfs' directions, and late that afternoon Matterhorn and the Baron were crouched in the heather a hundred feet from Karn's Trading Post. Broc eyed the establishment and gave a dismissive whinny.

The squat log building had an overhanging sod roof that gave it the appearance of a giant mushroom. Rough wooden crates and iron-hooped barrels cluttered the wraparound porch. Black pots and cast-iron skillets hung from ceiling hooks. Burlap sacks lounged against the walls. Strips of jerky festooned the open windows, attracting flies by the swarm. A pod of plump pickles swam in a brine vat near the door.

Except for a few skinny chickens and a tethered goat, the compound looked deserted.

"Let's go," the Baron said, slapping Matterhorn on the back. As they approached, they heard a wooden mill wheel paddling a spirited stream. The smell of dill filled the air.

"What's a leprechaun doing running a trading post?" Matterhorn asked. "I thought they were solitary creatures who avoided humans and hoarded gold."

"They will end up that way because of how people treated them," the Baron answered. "The big always take advantage of the small, and the small either adapt or perish. When Ireland becomes more populated, the leprechauns will learn they have to hide to survive."

Speaking of leprechauns, one came out of the door holding a shoe in one hand and a cobbler's hammer in the other. The rat-faced little man was a few inches shorter than Ian. He had pinched features and BB eyes. Shy wisps of cornsilk hair poked out from his narrow-brim derby hat. His large ears stuck to his scalp at the top and flapped loose at the bottom. He had a black olive mouth between his pointy nose and hairless chin.

Broc lowered his head and looked the leprechaun up and down. He took a few steps closer and gave the fellow a thorough sniffing. Then he swung his neck around and pushed Matterhorn back the way they had come.

Matterhorn resisted and said, "Calm down, Broc. We just want to ask the man a few questions."

Broc snorted and swished Matterhorn with his tail before trotting off.

The leprechaun ignored the snub and said in a reedy voice, "Ye must be Matterhorn and the Baron. I've been expectin' ye."

The Baron and Matterhorn looked at each other in surprise. Had the dwarfs double-crossed them and sent word of their escape? They didn't know what to say.

The leprechaun came to the edge of the porch. "My uncle said ye might show up. He told me to help ye any way I could. Name's Karn." When he spoke, the little man's rancid breath pushed the visitors back.

Matterhorn coughed out a, "Yell-O."

"Likewise," the Baron managed. "King Ian is the only leprechaun we've met since we've been here. Is he your uncle?"

Karn nodded.

"Doesn't that make you some sort of royalty?" Matterhorn said.

"If it did, I wouldn't be a shopkeeper," Karn spat out. The knuckles on his hammer hand went white.

"Do you own that mill?" the Baron asked, hitching his thumb toward the river.

"The farmers round here built it. I manage it."

"Does it have a grinding wheel?"

"Aye, there's a wheel next to the large millstones. The farmers use it to sharpen their tools."

"That's not all it's been used to sharpen," Matterhorn said. He untied the bone bomb from his pack and handed it to Karn, who put down his shoe and hammer.

"I've never seen the like of it," Karn said. "Where'd ye get it?"

"It came special delivery," the Baron said. "Airborne. Any idea who might have sent it?"

"No," the leprechaun said, almost dropping the bone. He gave it back to Matterhorn and began wiping his hands on his apron, his slender fingers a blur of motion.

The gesture reminded Matterhorn of Sherlock Holmes' number one rule of criminal detection, "Always look at the hands first, Watson." Karn was definitely nervous about something.

"Have there been any strangers around?" the Baron pressed. "Like the one who told you to set a pack of dwarfs on our trail. I don't think that's what your uncle had in mind when he said to help us."

Karn stepped back, stumbled, and caught his balance. His sharp gaze flitted from one tall outlander to the other. "It was just a business deal," he stammered. "I didn't want no part of it, but I couldn't afford to anger a man like—" he stopped and glanced around.

"Like who?" Matterhorn demanded.

"Like Bonehand."

"We've had about enough of this Bonehand character," the Baron said in disgust. "We've got a score to settle with this one-handed menace and some stolen property to recover. Do you know where we can find him?"

"He keeps to himself," Karn said. "But he comes here sometimes to buy supplies. Ye can wait till he shows up if ye want."

"And when might that be?"

"Don't know. But you'll never be findin' him in these woods." Sweeping his arm in a circle, Karn said, " 'Tis his front yard and most of the animals act like his pets. They pretty much do what he tells 'em."

I wonder if that applies to birds, Matterhorn thought. Especially ones large enough to carry deadly cargo.

Low thundering in the distance drew the Baron's attention to the graying horizon. The threat of rain caused him to ask Karn about a dry place to bed down for the night.

"There's a storage building by the mill," Karn offered. "We'll take it."

A bevy of white swans graced the millpond where Matterhorn and the Baron fished for their supper. They enjoyed spit-roasted trout garnished with onions and fresh greens from Karn's garden, thanks to Matterhorn taking over the cooking after the Baron burnt the first two fish to cinders.

They enjoyed a stream-bath before heading to the storage building. The tall, two-story structure was built of stone blocks that were stained moss green on the outside and wheat-dust yellow on the inside. The ground floor served as a stable—a fact Karn had failed to mention—so the guests decided to sleep upstairs.

The stalls were empty, but the place was not completely deserted. Reddish brown insects with yellow stripes buzzed around a giant gray spitball wadded above the large double doors. Pointing to the hornets' nest, the Baron said, "Those things don't lose their stingers when they attack. They can pop you like a nail gun."

The tremor in his voice made Matterhorn ask, "Are you speaking from experience?"

"A near-death experience," Aaron said as he slipped back outside.

Lofty Dream

MATTERHORN did not want to spend another night on the cold ground. "What are you afraid of?" he asked Aaron.

Slamming the door behind them, Aaron said, "I spend my summers at my grandpa's ranch. I love the place and everything about the country." He rubbed his shoulder and added, "Well, almost everything. Grandma hangs the wash on a clothesline in the yard to dry. One morning I climbed into my jeans and found they were already occupied. The hornet stung me eight times before I could de-pants myself."

Matterhorn chuckled as he pictured Aaron hopping around wildly swatting himself.

"You laugh," the Baron scolded, "but I had an allergic reaction and almost died. The last thing I need is to get stung out here in the boonies."

"Getting stung in the boonies sounds painful," Matterhorn quipped.

"Stick a few of those buzzers in your britches and see for yourself."

"No, thanks," Matterhorn declined. "For a great adventurer you don't seem very comfortable with nature," he teased.

"I can hold my own," the Baron retorted. "I just don't like creatures that bite or sting."

"Tell you what, we can use the side door and not disturb the residents." This they did, making their way carefully to the stout ladder, watching both the ground and the air for surprises. They climbed to a spacious loft strewn with freshly cut hay. The delicious smell of yellow sunshine and green fields wafted from the straw as they mounded it into fluffy mattresses.

The hayloft was occupied by a family of field mice who lived beyond the reach of Karn's cat. The feline security guard refused to climb and left them alone. The mice didn't mind the human company and Matterhorn soon had one of them eating out of his hand. The fuzzy creature reminded him of Reepicheep, his pet hooded rat. Reepicheep lived in a complex of plastic boxes and tubes that sprawled under Matterhorn's bed and into his closet. Matterhorn hoped someone was feeding Reep while he was gone.

Thinking of his room with its carpet-patch floor and poster-plastered walls made him homesick. Closing his eyes he could imagine his bass guitar propped by the cinder-block-and-pine bookshelves across from his bed. The top plank held his stereo, CDs, and several harmonicas. The second shelf hosted the works of Sir Arthur Conan Doyle, including his four novels and fifty-six short stories about

Sherlock Holmes. Holmes was Matterhorn's favorite character in all fiction.

The remaining shelves boasted books on everything from astronomy to zoology.

Ever since he was eight, Matterhorn had made it a rule to read one book a week. In the summers he read more. He found the people in books far more interesting than the ones on TV. His comic book collection, given to him by his dad, rested in neat piles underneath the bottom shelf. Its most valuable pieces were still cocooned in plastic.

A list of famous redheads was pinned above his desk to inspire him. The list included several presidents such as George Washington and Thomas Jefferson. Writers like Shakespeare and Mark Twain. World-changers like Galileo and Christopher Columbus and Napoleon.

So, what was this redhead doing lying on a pile of scratchy hay centuries from his soft bed? His sore ribs made it hard to get comfortable and reminded him that traveling was dangerous business. He glanced over at the Baron, who was picking his teeth with a twig. "What would've happened to me if those dwarfs had killed you?" he asked.

"Ever thought of being a farmer?"

"No. Would I have been stuck here the rest of my life?"

The Baron laughed. "Queen Bea would send someone to look for us if we didn't return. It might have taken a while to find you, though. How about shepherding? Do you like being outdoors?"

"I like being home," Matterhorn said. "We do get to go home once this is over, don't we?"

"After we accomplish our mission."

"Will we remember everything?"

"Yes."

That was a relief to Matterhorn. "Can you teach me to use that Cube of yours just in case?" he asked.

"It's pretty complicated," the Baron said, holding up the misshapen device. "First you have to triangulate the nearest portal with your desired time-space coordinates and then—"

"Never mind," Matterhorn said as the Baron's fingers flew around the gem-studded globe too fast to follow. "Just don't get yourself killed."

"It's nice to know you care."

"How did you get started with time travel in the first place?" Matterhorn asked. "Did you get sucked into it like me?"

Laying the Cube on his chest and folding his hands behind his neck, Aaron said, "I was recruited through a video game. It was the summer I got stung by the hornet. I always stayed at the ranch when mom had to go back to the city. Grandpa let me follow him around during the day. He taught me about machinery and how to fix things. At night we played video games together. He was pretty good for an old guy.

"One Saturday it was raining and I was bored. Grandpa had to go to town for feed, but before he left he handed me a game called *Travelers*. I'd never seen it before. You had to find these hidden portals and use them to collect artifacts from different time periods without getting caught. I got pretty good at it. Learned a lot about history along the way. Anyway, one day I got the bright idea there might be deeper levels to the game."

Matterhorn guessed where the story was headed but didn't interrupt.

"I thought the portals might be connected somehow," Aaron continued with a hint of pride. "I went looking for a hub and found it several nights later. And when my character stepped into the Hall of Portals, I became him."

"Were you as shocked as I was?" Matterhorn asked.

"I suppose so," the Baron replied. "Particularly about becoming an adult. That took some getting used to. I didn't meet the Queen until a few trips later. One of the Praetorians, those are the guardians you saw in the Propylon, explained traveling to me and I signed on."

"What do you know about First Realm?" Matterhorn asked.

"Not much," the Baron said. I've never been outside the Propylon. The Praetorians tell me Earth is a mirror world of First Realm. That's why we're so similar."

They talked a bit longer until last night's lack of sleep caught up to them and pulled them under. A few hours later, Matterhorn was enjoying a family camping trip in a lucid dream. His dad sat against a tree reading a book. Christy, his dog, chased butterflies across a mountain meadow. Matterhorn played catch with his older brother, Vic, and threw pinecones at his younger sister, Louise.

The weather in his dream warmed from balmy to blazing and Matterhorn kicked off his blanket. Sweat began pouring down his face. He watched in horror as his family melted like wax candles. The evergreens turned brown and burst into flames. Smoke stung his eyes and throat.

Above the snap-crackling inferno he heard a woman's voice cry, "You are in grave danger!"

The shrill warning shattered his nightmare and startled Matterhorn awake. He sat up into a dense cloud of acrid smoke; then fell back in a fit of coughing.

The loft was on fire!

Fire Escape

MATTERHORN'S loud hacking woke the Baron. "We've got trouble!" he coughed. Together they crawled to the edge of the loft and peered down. Bales of hay had been stacked beneath their perch and set ablaze. Wild orange flames cackled up at them. Intense heat slapped their faces and answered their unspoken question.

There was no way down.

No way out.

Whoever planned this barbecue had done a good job of trapping them on the grill.

"Follow the water to its source!" said the female voice that had awakened Matterhorn. They both heard it this time, but neither saw the speaker. A streamlet of water flowed through the straw toward them and poured over the edge to be vaporized by the heat. Matterhorn obeyed and moved into the wet with the Baron on his heels. They snagged their packs and boots as they slithered to the back of the loft.

By now their eyes were smoked shut. Matterhorn banged his head into the wall. A good thing he had thick hair to pad the blow. He squinted up to discover water pouring down from the window eight feet above. It was their only way out—if they could reach it.

Aaron the Baron also saw the opening. Filling his lungs with what little air he could find near the floor he knelt and made a stirrup. He motioned for Matterhorn to step up and then hoisted him to the broad windowsill. Next, he tossed up the packs before hauling himself up Matterhorn's down-stretched arm.

The strain on Matterhorn's ribs was almost more than he could bear.

They were on the river side of the building, and, despite gravity, there was a reverse waterfall climbing up the stones. Matterhorn braced himself and squeezed his eyes shut. He was afraid of heights and the twenty-foot drop made him dizzy. The Baron had no such qualms; he launched Matterhorn into space and followed him down.

Their clothes hissed when they landed in the water. Upon surfacing, they saw the one who had saved their lives. An exquisite young woman hovered in the mist above the churning mill wheel. Shoulder-length tawny hair outlined a porcelain doll face with blue eyes, soft cheeks, and a delicate chin. Moonlight glimmered off the aqua gown draping her trim figure. A shell-pink pearl dangled from each ear and an even larger bead hung around her throat on a strand of gold. She had pearl rings on several fingers and nail polish that matched her dress.

"Are you all right?" she asked in her silvery voice.

"Yeah, thanks to you!" shouted Matterhorn above the din. "We owe you our lives."

"So you do," she said. A coy smile played across her thin lips. Then her petite frame melted into the mist and her pearls plunked into the water.

Matterhorn tried to grab one and missed. "Who was that?" he asked the Baron.

"A naiad."

"What's a naiad?"

"A water nymph," the Baron answered as he tied his boots to his pack strap. He kicked away from the burning building into midstream.

Matterhorn followed. "So water nymphs are real here, too."

"They're real everywhere. They just don't show themselves very often. A good thing for us this one did." He scanned what could be seen of the riverbank in the firelight. Other than the fleeting outline of a small horse, nothing else moved. Whoever had set the fire hadn't waited around to see the outcome.

"Let's float downriver," the Baron said, "then circle back when things cool off to search for clues."

Although a strong swimmer, Matterhorn had trouble with his heavy pack until the Baron said, "See this tab?" He pointed to a small square on the pack's yellow rubber liner. "Pull it." With an inrush of air the backside of the pack expanded. "I attached a self-inflating airbag in the unlikely event of a water landing."

This guy is ready for anything, Matterhorn thought. And, for the first time since the fire, he remembered the one piece of equipment he was responsible for—the Sword! He felt for the hilt at his side and was relieved to find that the jump hadn't torn it off. It was stuck to the scritch pad on his belt. Relieved, he rolled onto his back and rested his head on the pack. As the current carried him along, he looked back at the burning building blowing smoke rings into the night sky. "Lucky for us the water nymph came by," he said at last.

"I don't believe in luck," the Baron proclaimed from a few feet away. "Nothing happens by chance. The Maker sees to that."

"We would've been shrimps on the barbie without the naiad," Matterhorn went on. "How did she do that? Get water up through the window and all?"

"Naiads can do anything with water," the Baron said. "It's what they're made of."

"How can someone be made of water?" Matterhorn scooped up a handful of river and let it run through his fingers.

"It's not so unusual. Our bodies are mostly water."

"That may be true," Matterhorn agreed, "but *this* body is ready to be dry again."

They had floated a fair distance by now and when the Baron spotted a red glow on the far shore he said, "Race you to that campfire."

"What if that's the arsonist?" Matterhorn said.

The Baron's eyes narrowed. "Then we'll teach him not to play with matches."

Helping Hand

AARON won the race to shore because of Matter-horn's sore chest. Together they shivered their way toward the stranger sitting with his back to the water and his face to the fire. The man had a dark woolen cloak draped over his large frame. The hood was down and a ponytail hung over his shoulder. He spoke without turning. "Do you always swim in your clothes?"

"Just doing our laundry," The Baron joked, shaking himself like a dog. "Can you spare some heat?"

The man nodded at the fire.

The Baron and Matterhorn approached and dropped their packs. They turned themselves slowly in the warmth while their host studied them with cat-green eyes.

Matterhorn stared back at the open, clean-shaven face unwrinkled by laugh lines. The man was well groomed compared to the dwarfs and leprechauns they had met so far. He had the lean features and musky odor of someone who lived outdoors. Matterhorn was good at guessing people's ages; he pegged this guy in his late twenties.

The pastel scent of chamomile spluttered from a teapot whistling to itself in the coals. Observing the code of the road, the man said in a gravelly voice, "Help yourselves. Meat, too, if you're hungry." He pointed with his chin to a line of sausages sizzling in a frying pan.

"Thanks," the Baron said. He dug two tin cups from his gear and held them while Matterhorn used the tail of his shirt as a potholder and poured. "Rather late for supper, isn't it?" he commented.

"I'm a night person. This is breakfast."

While waiting for his tea to cool, the Baron found a stick and stabbed a sausage. He offered it to Matterhorn; then speared one for himself. "Umm, these are good," he mumbled. "Crunchy on the outside and chewy on the inside. Is this venison or pork?"

"Caterpillar," the man said.

Aaron spat out what he hadn't swallowed and rinsed his mouth with scalding tea. Matterhorn laughed so hard that he almost choked. When he regained control he said to the cook, "These are pretty good. They need a little salt, though, and maybe a dab of horseradish."

Where food was concerned, Matterhorn would try anything once. His parents had taught him to treat food with an open mind and a discerning palate. He'd eaten everything from sushi to chocolate-covered grasshoppers.

While the Baron scraped his tongue with his front teeth, Matterhorn reached for another crispy critter. "These remind me of calamari," he said.

"What's that?" the man asked.

"Squid. You should try it next time you get to the coast. I assume you're not a local or you wouldn't be out here. Where are you from?"

"Around," said the caped figure. Only his face and well-worn boots were visible outside the dark folds of his garment. Neither gave a clue to his origin.

"Well, you need to be careful," Matterhorn advised. "Someone around here doesn't like strangers." He glanced at the wispy smoke in the distance that could have been his funeral pyre.

The man followed Matterhorn's gaze. "That's Karn's place. Did you two have anything to do with that?"

"We were sleeping in the stable," Matterhorn replied. "Someone tried to burn us alive."

"Were there animals inside?"

"No, thank goodness," the Baron said. He did not voice the main question on his mind—What were you doing about an hour ago?—but he did ask, "Have you seen anyone go by?"

"I haven't been here that long." The man swigged his tea from a pewter cup and added, "You're foreigners; I don't recognize your accents. Where are *you* from?"

"Around," the Baron said, being as vague as his host.

"Fair enough," the man replied. "Do you know who wants you dead?"

Matterhorn wrung water from his ponytail and answered, "We've got a pretty good idea, but catching him will be a major chore in these woods."

"Want some help?"

"That's a kind offer, but no," the Baron said. "Your hospitality has been help enough. This is our fight. We won't put anyone else in danger. By the way, my name's Aaron and this is Matterhorn." He leaned forward and extended his hand.

The man stared at the Baron's open palm for a long time before deciding how to respond. Then he slowly drew his right hand from under his cloak.

It had no flesh on it.

The Baron jerked away as if from a corpse. Matterhorn jumped up and had his Sword leveled at Bonehand's chest in the blink of an eye. But Bonehand didn't blink. He simply said, "Do you always show your appreciation with the point of a blade?"

"We don't appreciate people trying to kill us," Matterhorn said, his eyes boring into Bonehand's.

Bonehand gave a short laugh. "If I wanted you dead, we wouldn't be having this conversation." His words did not have the tinny ring of boast or threat. They came across as a simple fact.

"Are you saying you're not responsible for what's been happening to us?" the Baron demanded.

"Such as?"

"The bone bomb, and the kidnappers, not to mention tonight's fire. You had nothing to do with those?"

Bonehand extended his good left hand and touched the Sword of Truth. "I swear I've not tried to kill you."

This brazen act stunned Matterhorn and the Baron.

Bonehand grinned at their startled faces. "I saw you use this on the dwarfs."

Lowering the blade, Matterhorn said, "If you didn't send them, how did you know about the kidnapping?"

"I make it my business to know what goes on in my forest."

"Do you know why we're here?" the Baron asked.

"To find Ian's Flute."

"Ian thinks you took it," Matterhorn said.

"He's wrong."

"Karn told us you hired the dwarfs," the Baron added.

"He lied."

"It's your word against his."

Bonehand stirred the fire and sent a fountain of sparks skyward. "If you paid more attention to facts than rumors, you'd know who was telling the truth." He watched the flicks of amber rise and blink away.

The Baron and Matterhorn sat down and waited.

At last Bonehand spoke. "There's a common thread in your troubles."

Matterhorn did a flash review of the last few days. They were anything but common. What had he missed? When he asked Bonehand, the man clicked off several points on his bare digits.

Click. "I heard what you said about the bone that fell from the sky, how it was sharpened by a millstone. Who runs the only mill for miles around?"

"Karn," Matterhorn said, trying not to stare at the skeletal visual aid.

Click. "Who did the dwarfs say would pay them for getting rid of you?"

"Karn," the Baron answered.

Click. "Whose building did you almost die in tonight?"

"Karn, again," Matterhorn said. He snapped a twig into tiny pieces and tossed them into the short flames. "The leprechaun's got a sneaky face," Matterhorn admitted. "But we've never even met until today. What could he possibly have against us?"

Click. Bonehand thumbed his little finger against the others. "You're after what he's got."

Duo to Trio

"KARN'S got the Flute!" Aaron cried. He was leaning so intently forward by now that his forearms slid off his knees and he lost his balance.

Bonehand drew his hands to his lips and pretended to play the wondrous whistle.

Matterhorn could see Bonehand's logic, but he had trouble with Karn's. "Why would Karn steal from his own family?"

"Money and power," Bonehand said. "His father is Ian's younger brother, which puts him close enough to royalty to smell it, but not close enough to taste it. His cousins are princes, but he's a struggling trader. I'd bet my good hand someone offered him a pretty price for the Flute."

"How come Ian suspects you and not his nephew?" the Baron pressed.

"For the same reason you suspected me," Bonehand said. "I disagree with Ian about the Flute. I keep to myself. I dress funny. I have a deformity"—he held up his hand and rattled the bones—"therefore I'm evil, right?"

The Baron and Matterhorn looked at each other sheepishly. "I guess we misjudged you because of your reputation," Matterhorn admitted.

"Yeah," the Baron agreed, although he still felt uneasy about this dark stranger.

Bonehand shrugged. "I'm used to it. People think they know what a person's like by looking at his skin. When it's different colored or damaged in some way they assume the worst. They never bother to check." He smirked and added, "I get blamed for everything from lightning fires to lost sheep."

"Our apologies for blaming you," Matterhorn said. He stood and offered Aaron a hand up. "I guess we've got a Karn to catch."

"It's too late for that tonight," Bonehand said. "The lep probably took off the minute he set fire to the stable. You'll have to wait till morning to track him."

"He's right," Aaron said. "Besides, I'm tired. Mind if we bed down here?"

Just then, a rustling noise sounded in the dark. The Sword came out, but was put away when Broc trotted into view. Matterhorn gave his four-footed friend a two-armed hug around the neck and rubbed the broccoli birthmark. "Glad to see you found us, Broc."

Aaron fished a candy bar from his pack and tossed it to Matterhorn, who barely got the wrapper off before Broc inhaled the treat.

"Well, I'll be," Bonehand said, more surprised to see the horse than he had been to see Matterhorn and the Baron. "Do you know who this is?"

"I don't know his real name," Matterhorn replied. "I call him Broccoli, er, I mean, Broc."

"He's not a vegetable!" Bonehand said. "He's a noble scion, a direct descendant of Chiron the Wise, the centaur who tutored Jason and Achilles."

"Broc was wise enough not to trust Karn," the Baron said. "He tried to warn us but we didn't listen."

Bonehand studied the steed from hoof to forelock in the flickering light. The animal was a living work of art, perfect in line and proportion. "We are fortunate to have his company," Bonehand said in a reverent tone. "Not many of his kind are left in the world. Their bodies are entirely equine now; they can no longer speak. Still, their minds are as developed as humans. I've seen this one in the forest before, but never as close. I'm amazed he lets you touch him."

"Touch him," Matterhorn said. "I've ridden him."

"You may be the only person who has," Bonehand said. "No offense, but it has more to do with the Sword you carry than with you."

Broc neighed and shook his head. He stepped closer to Matterhorn and touched the hilt with his nose. The blade lit up in response.

The gesture brought a smile to Bonehand's face. "If this animal trusts you, I guess I can, too. You're welcome to my fire. And my help."

"We'll take the first," the Baron said, "but like I said before, we won't need the help."

"I'm not asking," Bonehand said, "I'm telling. I'll not let the Flute be used to harm innocent animals. I warned Ian this would happen. It has to be stopped."

"We can't involve you in—"

"I know these woods," Bonehand interrupted, "and you don't. I also know how to use this." He drew back his cloak to reveal a short sword of exquisite workmanship. The handle was wrapped in faded blue leather and capped with a bronze pommel. Bonehand drew out the blade. The edges of the gray shaft were sharpened to a silver gleam.

Matterhorn let out a low whistle. "Where'd you get that?"

"I found it in the cave where I first hid as a child."

"It looks Roman," Matterhorn said. "Their legions were in these parts centuries ago. Can I see it?'

Bonehand let the sword drop back into its sheath. "Look at it in the morning."

Aaron realized there was nothing he and Matterhorn could do. The duo had just become a trio. Counting Broc, they were actually a quartet. Glancing at the horse in profile gave Aaron an idea. His best thoughts often came like that, as bolts of inspiration. Taking off his belt, he held it in front of him and approached Broc. "If you are who this man says, you can understand me, right?"

Broc nodded.

"You know what we're here for, then," the Baron continued. "We think Karn has Ian's Flute. He'll have to play it sooner or later to prove to a potential buyer that it's the real thing. When that happens, will you have to obey its call?"

Another nod.

The Baron's hunch was right. "There's a tracking device in my belt. If I put it around your neck we can follow you and protect you. Is that okay?"

Broc snorted and lowered his head. The belt just fit around his powerful neck. "This will send out a signal for up to three days," Aaron said, activating the beacon. "Something's bound to happen before then." He went to his pack and switched off the beeping noise coming from the homing device. He checked to make sure the green light was blinking in the center of the compact screen.

"Don't worry," Matterhorn said, coming up and rubbing Broc behind the ears. "We won't let anything happen to you."

"Enough for tonight," the Baron said.

Since his bedroll had been lost in the fire, he covered himself with a wool poncho and was soon snoring quietly.

Matterhorn had too much on his mind to sleep. "Can I ask you a question?" he said to Bonehand. "I've seen you tend the fire and tidy up. How is it you can use your bone hand so well?"

Flexing his naked fingers, Bonehand said, "The muscles that work the fingers are in the forearm. Tendons connect them to the bones. My skin was broiled in the fire, but most of the tendons survived. Gradually I've trained myself to use my hand again. It's not pretty, but it works."

Bonehand noticed Matterhorn's gaze sliding up to the goo leaking from around his shirt cuff. "I make this salve from herbs and honey," he explained. "It prevents infection and keeps the tendons lubricated."

"I admire your grit," Matterhorn said. "But tell me, do you regret trying to save those animals?"

"Not a bit," Bonehand said instantly. "I'd do it again if I had to. I can't stand to see animals suffer."

Matterhorn wanted to ask about the soldiers who had started the fire, but Bonehand turned away and pulled the hood over his head.

Follow the Leader

MATTERHORN, Broc, the Baron, and Bonehand hid in the trees watching a group of farmers poke around the burned building next to the mill. Ghostly dust devils swirled in the morning breeze flush with fresh charcoal. One of the men came out of the smoldering ruin with a silvery sheet in his hand. "Someone must've been in the stable last night."

Matterhorn mouthed the words, "Your blanket."

"The fire was set on purpose," said a second farmer holding up the butt-end of a blackened torch.

"Anyone find any bones in the ashes?" another asked.

Several shook their heads or grunted, "No."

"Karn's gone!" a lad yelled across the clearing from the porch of the trading post. "The hearth's cold and his bed ain't been slept in!"

"Foul play," said the first speaker knowingly.

"Bonehand's work," muttered a middle-aged man leaning on his pitchfork. "The sooner we get rid of 'im the safer we'll all be."

Bonehand gave Matterhorn and the Baron an "I told you so" look.

The farmers drew themselves into a tight knot of concern. "Those who can spare a man or two, send 'em back here in an hour," came a crisp command from the center. "And make sure they're well armed. We'll scour the woods till we catch the blackguard this time."

When the way was clear, Matterhorn and the others made their own quick search for clues. "There was a skiff by the millpond yesterday," he said after circling the area. "It's gone."

"Which means Karn's headed for the coast," Bonehand said. "It's thirty miles and he'll make better time on the water than we can on land. Once he reaches the shore, we won't know if he's gone north or south."

"The best we can do is follow and wait for him to use the Flute," the Baron said. He shaded his eyes and glanced skyward. "It's 9:15 now; we've got a long day ahead of us. Let's go."

Walking beside their new guide, Matterhorn got a chance to study the mystery man in the light of day. At five foot six, he was a head shorter than his new companions. His black hair was drawn back from his forehead and ears, giving his face a severe look. He had high cheekbones and straight, but dingy, teeth. An intricate pewter broach fastened the sleek cloak at the neck. Underneath he wore a dark linen shirt and buckskin breeches tucked into high boots. His stride was easy and confident.

In contrast to Bonehand's subdued outfit, the countryside blossomed with bluebells, blackthorns, butterburs, and primroses. Every green-crested hill seemed to have a frisky brook playing down one side or the other. Farther away, thickset stonewalls separated the velour pastures of well-kept farms. Pheasants occasionally fluttered from field to field in bursts of feathery excitement.

Under different circumstances, Matterhorn would have loved to talk to the people who owned those farms. His grandfather, a man he respected for his faith and wisdom, had come from Irish stock. But Matterhorn knew he would be seen as an accomplice of the man in black, who was no doubt suspected of every unsolved crime in the district.

Aaron's horse had never returned and Matterhorn chose not to ride Broc, so they progressed at foot-speed. To pass the time Matterhorn tried to learn more about Bonehand. "What's your real name, if you don't mind me asking?"

"Bonehand will do," came the terse reply.

"You don't sound Irish"

"That's because I'm English."

Remembering what Ian had said about Bonehand's parents, Matterhorn tried a different approach. "I'm sorry about your folks being killed. Do you have any other family?"

"None worth talking about."

"So you live alone?"

"I have a forest full of friends."

"Does that include the leprechauns?"

"Some."

"How long have you known Ian?"

"Years."

"Do you ever visit the nearby towns?"

Bonehand glowered as if the question was too dumb to deserve an answer. "Do you ever stop talking?"

Matterhorn snapped his jaw shut. Just as well; Bonehand might begin asking questions of his own. Matterhorn wouldn't lie and Bonehand wouldn't believe he was a kid from the future given an adult body and sent by the Queen of First Realm to find one of the Ten Talis. Matterhorn hardly believed it himself.

They moved over the next several hills in silence. An easterly breeze kicked up and brought with it a faraway snapping sound. From the top of the next rise they spotted a farmer at the plow. He was using a bullwhip on the slow-footed draft horse in harness. The huge creature shuddered under the rain of blows. His legs strained against the burden of the dull blade. Blood ran down his sweaty sides from the gashes on his back.

The sight was enough to throw Bonehand into a towering rage. He ran to the end of the field and vaulted the rock hedge. The farmer lashed his horse again before turning to face the caped intruder. He was a head taller than Bonehand and broader in the shoulders. He seemed put out by this interruption, but not afraid.

"Should we do something?" Matterhorn asked the Baron.

"Like what?" Aaron replied. They stopped at the wall and watched.

"How would you fancy the lash on your own back?" Bonehand barked.

"Keep yer nose outta my business or I'll peel it off," the man retorted, shaking his whip.

Bonehand ignored the threat and kept coming.

The farmer's face got hard. He drew back his hand and snapped the seven-foot cord forward faster than the eye could follow.

Bonehand raised his right arm and let the leather snake coil itself around his forearm. Then he grabbed it with his bony fingers and yanked the weapon free. He caught the hilt in his left hand and a moment later was chasing the surprised farmer toward the barn. He landed several lashes, and might have seriously injured the man if the race hadn't been abruptly ended by the barn door.

Bonehand slid a board through the brackets and locked the farmer inside. He flung the whip down the well. Returning to the field he cut the horse loose and led him toward the gate near Matterhorn and the Baron.

He didn't look back and so didn't see the farmer appear in the loft opening with a longbow in his hands. His chest heaved with exertion as he fitted arrow to string and took careful aim.

When the Baron saw the farmer, he reached into his pocket and drew out a compact signal mirror. He unfolded it and directed a flash of sunlight into the man's face just as he fired. He flinched and sent the arrow high of its target and into the wall just below the Baron's waist.

"Hurry up!" Matterhorn screamed at Bonehand.

Aaron blinded the farmer each time he raised his bow. Finally, it dawned on him to back away from the opening and shoot, but by then Bonehand and the horse were safely among the trees.

Not wanting any more trouble with the locals, the Baron suggested they follow the river from deeper in the woods, which suited Bonehand fine. He soon had them in timber so dense that Broc and the plow horse could barely squeeze through.

Matterhorn and the Baron trudged along behind the animals, watching where they stepped. "Quick thinking with the mirror," Matterhorn complimented his friend. "You saved Bonehand's life and he didn't even say thanks."

"He doesn't strike me as the kind who says thank you," Aaron replied.

"What do we really know about him?" Matterhorn said quietly. "Maybe he lied about Karn. Maybe he'll keep the Flute once we find it and kill us like he did those soldiers."

"He could have killed us last night," the Baron observed. "Let's not give him a reason to reconsider the idea."

Bounty Men

IT was after noon when they reached a clearing and stopped for lunch. The leafy boughs of the largest tree Matterhorn had ever seen overshadowed the entire glade. Thick limbs splayed from the massive trunk in all directions forming the rafters of the green roof. Gnarled roots dug into the ground like giant fingers.

Bonehand washed the draft horse's cuts and brushed the crusty blood from his coat. Broc paid no attention to the large brute since they had little in common. He chewed at the tender turf while the humans shared jerky and dried fruit. As they rested beneath the great tree, a gray squirrel scampered over the exposed roots and jumped into Bonehand's lap. He had a stick in his mouth that turned out to be the tip of an arrow.

"We've got company," Bonehand said. "And not far away."

This proved an understatement as just then an arrow thwacked into the wood an inch above Matterhorn's head.

A second arrow sliced through the air—and into Broc's right shoulder.

Matterhorn's panic at almost being killed was overwhelmed by his anger at seeing Broc hit. The horse was jolted sideways by the force of the blow and neighed in pain.

Ignoring the danger, Matterhorn started toward Broc, but the Baron grabbed his shirt and yanked him around the trunk. Bonehand dove around the other side a whisker ahead of another thirty-inch bolt of death.

"We've got to help Broc!" Matterhorn shouted as more arrows thunked into the tree. He raised his head and peeked over the root. He couldn't see the horses.

"There he goes," the Baron said, pointing to a break in the trees through which Broc's tail was disappearing at a gallop. He spun on Bonehand and cried, "It's the farmer's mob already!"

Bonehand shook his head. "Bounty men more likely."

"There's a price on your head?" Matterhorn sputtered. "Why didn't you tell us?"

Bonehand slipped off his cloak and rucksack. He handed them to Matterhorn and said, "It doesn't make a difference."

Throwing down the pack, Matterhorn snapped, "It does if someone's trying to kill us to collect!"

"Some soldiers disappeared after the big fire that took my hand," Bonehand said. "That's ancient history. Now, do what I say and you'll live to tell your children about this. Keep these yokels busy till I'm away; then run straight through there." He pointed to a wooded draw on the far side of the meadow. "You won't be followed; it's me that's worth a hundred pieces of gold." He crouched on the balls of his feet and studied the canopy overhead as he spoke.

"What about Broc?" Matterhorn demanded.

"Judging by his speed, he's not hurt bad," Bonehand replied. "The arrow must have hit a bone. He'll need that shaft removed, though. I'll see to it soon as I can."

Matterhorn wondered at Bonehand's confidence.

"A mile or so from here you'll come to a deep ravine," Bonehand continued. "Below will be the river. Follow it west to low ground."

"And what if—"

But Bonehand was already climbing upward as the squirrel had done when the attack began. His fingers gripped the coarse bark like claws.

"You heard the man," the Baron said. "Draw your Sword."

Matterhorn did so and Aaron draped Bonehand's cloak on the blade. When Matterhorn tilted the garment outward it attracted a hail of arrows.

"Why are you trying to kill us!" the Baron screamed at the attackers. "We've done nothing wrong!"

"Give us the man in black an' ye can go yer way," came a heavy brogue reply.

Matterhorn looked out the top of his eyes to see Bonehand's heels vanish among the leaves. "Let's make a deal!" Matterhorn shouted. "How about splitting the reward?"

"How 'bout we just kill the lot of ye?" came the answer, followed by another pointed volley.

The Baron dug into an inside pocket of his pack and produced a small red ball with a stubby green fuse. He knew what Bonehand would attempt and wanted to give him a fighting chance. He waited a few more moments before lighting the M-80—which had the punch of a quarter-stick of dynamite—and lobbing it toward the voice.

The Baron and Matterhorn covered their ears as the explosion rocked the clearing and filled the air with a caustic smell of gunpowder. Bonehand dropped from a branch thirty feet away and raced into a thicket of ash trees before the bounty men could regain their senses.

When they did, rather than expose themselves to unknown danger, they stayed on the fringe and worked around the meadow to catch Bonehand's trail.

Matterhorn caught glimpses of four men in jerkins, yew bows in their hands and goose-feathered shafts stuffed into their quivers. He prayed Bonehand's head start would be large enough, as a decent bowman could down a running deer at 200 yards.

Running is what he and the Baron did next—in the opposite direction. Bonehand's prediction proved mostly correct. They were not chased. However, one of the men stopped long enough to send an arrow after them, more out of frustration than malice. Had he taken time to aim properly, the missile would have found Matterhorn's back instead of zipping past his ear.

Matterhorn felt the fletching on his cheek and the sensation tripled his speed, which almost cost him his life. After running a few-minute mile, he beat the Baron to the ravine Bonehand had mentioned. It was actually a deep gouge in the earth that plummeted two hundred feet from a shear cliff to a cauldron of churning rapids.

Matterhorn broke through the thick brush hiding the edge, his feet churning, cartoon-like, in midair.

Cliff-hanger

THE foliage that masked the sheer drop is what actually saved Matterhorn's life, for as he fell, he managed to spin and grab a skein of sturdy roots. The weight of his body and pack stretched his arms. His shoulders popped painfully, but his grip held.

The Baron skidded to a halt when Matterhorn disappeared in front of his eyes. "Matterhorn!" he cried. "Matterhorn!"

"Stay back!" Matterhorn warned.

"Where are you?"

"Down here!" Ten feet away a bush rustled. The Baron dropped to his stomach and inched forward. Brambles clawed at his clothes and skin. He reached the edge and looked down.

Matterhorn twisted in space. His face had gone white as his teeth, which were clenched as tightly as his fingers.

Aaron curled his legs around a stout bush and extended himself over the edge. He put one pack strap in the crook of his elbow and lowered the other toward Matterhorn. "Grab on!" he cried.

Matterhorn stared at the loop a few feet away. He told his right hand to let go of the root and grab the strap, but it wouldn't obey.

The Baron crawled a few inches forward and balanced his weight on the knife-edge. "Now!"

Matterhorn said a silent prayer then arched upward in a desperate lunge and caught the strap. He pawed at the dirt wall in front of him with his feet and free hand for traction. When he made it to flat ground, he and the Baron crawled away from the ravine and collapsed back-to-back.

Matterhorn's breath came in raggedy gasps. The Baron started to laugh in sheer relief.

"What's so funny?" Matterhorn croaked.

"You should have seen your face," he replied. "You looked like an albino rabbit."

"I just about died!" Matterhorn shot back. The ordeal had been particularly terrifying because of his fear of heights.

"Close, but no cigar. Remember what I told you about the Sword. You won't die as long as you're wearing it."

Bristling at the Baron's smugness, Matterhorn snapped, "What was it gonna do, turn into a parachute?"

"Perhaps it sharpened your senses so you could save yourself."

"Perhaps I should sharpen your senses." Matterhorn reached for the hilt at his waist. "Yeow, that hurts!" he cried, not knowing whether to grab his shoulder or his chest.

"Take it easy, partner," the Baron soothed. "You can teach me a lesson another day. We'd best get moving in case those archers decide to come after easier prey."

"I should be home reading about adventures, instead of having them," Matterhorn muttered. "In the past few days we've been bombed, kidnapped, set fire to, and shot at." He struggled to his feet.

"Beats being in school," Aaron said, dusting off his pants and adjusting his pack.

They followed the sun westward for hours and gradually made their way down to the river, where they stopped to rest.

Matterhorn had calmed down enough to be thankful for their narrow escape. "I hope Broc's okay," he said as he squatted and drank from his hand.

"And Bonehand," Aaron added, washing the cuts on his face.

Matterhorn picked stickers from his forearm and said, "He's getting what he deserves, but Broc's done nothing wrong." He remembered the look in the horse's eyes after being shot. He could see the arrow quivering in the muscular shoulder just below the Baron's belt.

"That's it!" Matterhorn cried, almost tumbling head-first into the stream. He straightened up and grabbed Aaron's arm. "We can use your tracking device to find Broc!"

"We could . . . ," the Baron said slowly, "but . . . there's no time. We're here to find the Flute. Karn may already be at the coast . . ."

"But Broc could bleed to death!"

"Hopefully Bonehand has found him. The sooner we get the Flute, the sooner we can go back for them."

"What's so important about the Talis?" Matterhorn exploded in frustration. "We've almost been killed several times. Broc may already be dead. Why doesn't the Maker get the Flute Himself? He must know where it is."

"That's not His way," the Baron said. "The Maker doesn't interfere like that. He's written a script, but sometimes people decide to run their own show. When that happens, He doesn't appear and fix everything. Instead He works through those who are true to Him to undo the damage and restore the story."

He put a hand on Matterhorn's shoulder and continued. "The Sword of Truth pulled you into this for a reason. Remember your oath and play your part with courage. What you and I do here will affect the outcome of history."

Matterhorn sighed. "That's too much responsibility."

"I said the Maker doesn't interfere; I didn't say He's not involved. He'll give us the help we need when we need it. He already has; that's why we're still alive."

"And fortunate to be so," said a familiar voice from behind a nearby bush.

"Your Majesty!" the Baron said in surprise. "Where'd you come from?"

"From searchin' fer me flute, where else?" Ian said as he stepped into view.

"Any luck?"

Ian shook his head.

"How did you find us?" Matterhorn asked.

The leprechaun tapped Matterhorn's boot with his shillelagh. "These leave a trail a near-sighted noodge could follow. Where ye be goin' in such a hurry?"

"We're trying to catch Karn."

"Karn?"

"Your nephew's headed to the coast with your Flute," the Baron said.

Ian gave them both a skeptical stare. "Karn has me Flute?"

"We think so," Matterhorn replied. "Or I should say, Bonehand thinks so."

"Bonehand! Have ye seen him?"

"Spent the day with him," the Baron quipped. "Delightful chap."

"Where's the rogue now?"

"Running for his life from bounty hunters," Matterhorn answered.

"Some angry farmers are after him as well," Aaron added. "They think he started the fire at the mill, but he didn't. He didn't hire the dwarfs that kidnapped me either."

"Great Honk!" Ian cried, slapping his forehead with his hand. "Bounty hunters, mad farmers, kidnappin' dwarfs, what have ye been up to the past few days?"

"Up to our armpits in piranhas," Matterhorn said, "but we're pressing on."

"Which we need to be doing," the Baron interjected, "if we're going to find the Flute. You're welcome to come with us," he invited Ian.

The leprechaun chewed his lower lip thoughtfully before declining. "Yer legs be too long. I'll make me own way." But he made no move to leave.

"Is there something else?" the Baron asked.

Ian cleared his throat. "Might I trouble ye for a wee bit more of the chocolate?" The gray hair in his mole quivered with anticipation.

"No trouble," the Baron said, fetching a packet of cocoa from his foodstuffs. "Mix the powder with hot water. Throw the wrapper in the fire when you're done."

The Baron and Matterhorn resumed their journey, walking until darkness made it too dangerous to continue. They pitched camp in a half-moon meadow and ate supper in silence—until a rustling sound from where the firelight frittered into the trees put them on full alert.

Bad Reputation

BROC!" Matterhorn cried, jumping up and running to the horse in spite of the Baron's warning to be careful. The noble steed favored his left front leg, which had a mash poultice on his shoulder where the arrow had struck. He tossed his mane in greeting and accepted a neck-rubbing from Matterhorn.

Bonehand walked past without a word and sat down at the fire next to the Baron. He wore his rucksack and cape and acted like nothing had happened. There were, however, three round holes in the woven fabric.

Poking a finger through one of these, the Baron asked, "You went back for this?"

"I sent a badger for it," Bonehand said. He lifted the hem to show a mouth-shaped set of punctures. "It gets cold in the forest at night."

The Baron peered in the direction Broc and Bonehand had come. "Any chance you were followed?"

"None."

"You're sure?" the Baron pressed. He offered Bone-hand a cup of cocoa.

Bonehand accepted the warm liquid but didn't bother to repeat his answer.

"I take it this isn't the first time you've been shot at."

Bonehand snorted and took a long drink. "It's the closest I've come to being hit. I was careless."

"Winston Churchill once said, 'There is nothing so exhilarating as being shot at without effect,'" Matterhorn quoted as he joined the conversation.

"Who's Churchill?"

"Never mind," Matterhorn said. "What about the bounty men?"

Bonehand folded his legs Indian-style beneath his cloak. "They won't be troubling us again."

"I don't get it," Matterhorn said, fearing the worst. "You care so much for animals and so little for humans. How can you just kill people without remorse?"

"Who said anything about killing?"

"But the bounty men—"

"—are halfway to Galway Bay on the trail I left them," Bonehand finished.

"Well," Matterhorn said, "what about the soldiers who set the fire that ruined your hand? They're dead, right?"

Bonehand nodded. "They died of stupidity."

"Ian told us you killed them," the Baron said.

"I'd have beaten the potatoes out of those vermin if I'd caught them," Bonehand said, "but I wouldn't have murdered them." He accepted a refill of cocoa before telling the rest of the story. "I tracked 'em through the blaze to a box canyon. They must've been drunk not to read the terrain. The fire swept through like a flood. I buried their charred bones when things cooled down. I wept for their horses, but not for them."

Matterhorn felt relieved not to be sitting knee-to-knee with a mass murderer. Still, he was confused. "If you didn't kill those men, why does everyone think you did?"

"Because I never said otherwise."

"You never tried to clear your name?"

"I've found that the darker my reputation, the fewer people come into these woods. It's better for the animals this way."

"But what about the price on your head?"

Bonehand laughed a genuine belly laugh. "It's all a game. The day a longbow yeoman can pin me is the day he's earned his prize money."

Again they had misjudged the man in black, Matterhorn realized. He pulled his shirt closer against the evening damp and changed the subject. "How much farther to the coast?"

"Twelve miles," Bonehand said without hesitation. "We can be there tomorrow afternoon."

The Baron got up and examined Broc's shoulder. He touched the hardened yellowish patch and said, "I've got an antibiotic for this."

"I've been tending animals for years," Bonehand said. "He's fine."

The Baron decided not to press it. Instead he patted Broc's flank and said, "Can you handle a dozen miles big boy?"

Broc reared on his hind legs and snorted a jet of steam into the cool air like a dragon.

"Don't patronize him," Bonehand warned as the Baron retreated a few paces.

"Broc may be rarin' to go," Matterhorn said, "but I need some rest."

"We can't all sleep," Aaron pointed out. "Someone has to watch Broc in case the Flute is played. Let's draw for the watch schedule." He snapped a piece of kindling in three and stuffed the twigs into his fist. "Short stick, first watch."

The Baron came up short, with Bonehand drawing second shift.

"Goooood," Matterhorn yawned. "I'm an early riser anyway. You know what they say; the early bird gets the worm."

The Baron grimaced. "If it tastes anything like caterpillar, you're welcome to it."

Matterhorn managed a few hours sleep before being awakened for his predawn watch by a pointy finger in the side.

"Careful," he muttered to Bonehand through chapped lips. "I'm bruised as an overripe banana."

"What's a banana?" Bonehand asked.

"A piece of fruit," Matterhorn said. He sat up sluggishly and accepted a cup of warm tea. "I hope this has some caffeine in it."

"What's caf—"

"Never mind," Matterhorn said grumpily.

After Bonehand was asleep, and before the sun was awake, Matterhorn saw the white horse he had spotted by the lake. Only now he could tell it wasn't a horse. The creature stood in a patch of moonlight across the river. Its perfectly formed body had been shaped for beauty rather than brawn. Its mane and plumed tail glinted with a reddish hue.

An eighteen-inch spike parted the silky hair on the unicorn's forehead.

The spiraling opal horn reminded Matterhorn of something he'd seen recently, but he couldn't quite put his finger on it.

Pirate Cove

SUNRISE found the unicorn gone and Matterhorn shivering over the remains of some dying coals. For the past hour, he'd been softly playing his harmonica as a sea mist rolled up the river valley like dry ice fog. The cobwebs in the bushes glittered with dew beads. A nest of robins announced the new morn.

Matterhorn rose and ambled toward the river to wash his face. He scanned the grassy field where Broc stood fast asleep. The horse hadn't twitched a muscle on his watch, but as Matterhorn passed, Broc's head jerked upright, his eyelids snapped open, and after a brief pause he cantered away.

"Hey, Broc," Matterhorn called, but the animal paid no attention.

Reaching the water, Broc veered right and vanished into the fog. Matterhorn couldn't hear anything, but he knew Ian's Flute was being played. He saw no one on either bank and guessed the musician was somewhere downstream.

"Come back!" Matterhorn yelled. This had no effect on Broc, but it roused the Baron and Bonehand. Within fifteen minutes they were packed and tuned in to the Baron's homing device.

"What's that thing?" Bonehand asked. He pointed at the blinking green light under the glass screen.

"It's like a compass," Aaron said, "but instead of pointing north, the green flash points to a piece of metal in my belt."

This was enough of an explanation for Bonehand. He made no effort to keep up with the ways of foreigners.

When the fog burned off later in the morning, the trackers were careful to keep out of sight. They didn't want to give themselves away until they knew who was playing the Flute. It was early afternoon when they topped a breezy knoll and saw the stream pour itself into a spacious bay.

Gigantic fingers of rock reached into the Atlantic on either side. Dingy seagulls and lanky herons fluttered over the ribbon of sand that separated green hills from blue waves. Down the beach, a band of shirtless men were lashing logs together into a large raft. Thinner logs had been roped together to form a makeshift corral that held several unusual animals—including Broc.

Next to Broc stood the unicorn from the night before. The rest of the animals in the enclosure were smaller. A handsome peacock preened his tail. Silent songbirds perched on the top rail as though glued there. Two coppery squirrels the size of Cheshire cats sat in one corner.

A few red foxes skittered about, black ears at attention and white-tipped tails swishing the air. They didn't bother the birds, which normally would have been on the menu for lunch.

Bonehand pulled Matterhorn to the ground next to him. "Keep out of sight," he hissed. He pointed toward the sea and Matterhorn saw a ship lounging at anchor. The twin-masted schooner was rigged with mainsail, foresail, and topsails. She also boasted a jib and a flying jib off the bowsprit.

The Baron groaned. "A ship that size will have a lot of hands," he said. "We only have five."

Bonehand gave him a hard look.

"I mean, six," Aaron corrected. He rolled onto his back and fished the signal mirror from his pocket. It was the size of a deck of cards until he unfolded its polished panels. He held this above the top of the hill, so he could see without being seen.

Matterhorn and Bonehand scrunched closer to watch the bayside action. They saw Karn in the middle of the scene, perched on the top rail of the corral with Ian's Flute hanging from a silver chain around his neck. He was arguing with a great white shark of a man who was obviously in charge.

The man was cut square as a ship's beam. His shoulders jutted out at right angles from a pug neck. He wore a white silk shirt, green velvet waistcoat, and loose trousers. The ivory-handled dagger on his right hip balanced the cutlass on his left. A tri-cornered hat sat rakishly on his head. Under its brim, bushy sideburns bracketed his brown face. Gold earrings dangled from each ear. His yellowed teeth had been filed to points, giving him a shark-like appearance when he sneered.

"I wish we could hear what they're saying," Matterhorn said.

"I can tell you that," Bonehand said. "I've seen these ships before. They come from Britain and prowl the coast in search of rare game and careless men. They sell the animals to the royal courts in Europe. The men they auction to merchants who can't get a ship's crew any other way."

"Pirates," Matterhorn concluded.

Below them, Karn was gesturing between the captain and the animals with the Flute.

"He's bickering over price," Bonehand said, resuming his commentary. "If he isn't careful, he'll get the point of a knife for payment."

"That raft is almost done," Matterhorn observed. "We can't let Broc and the animals be taken to the ship."

"Agreed," the Baron said. "But there are a dozen men onshore and who knows how many more on that boat. Our best shot at freeing the animals will be after dark."

"That's no good," Matterhorn countered. "There will be two moons tonight, the one in the sky and its reflection on the water. It will be impossible to sneak up on anybody. Besides, it might be too late by then."

But it was already too late.

"Fie!"

Chapter 26

WHILE Karn and the captain continued to argue, a great bird of prey dropped into the picture, landing on a post near them. The huge gyrfalcon was an impressive and powerful creature. Its five-foot wingspan had enabled it to deliver the bone that had almost killed the Baron.

The captain said something in answer to a shrill squawk and the bird took to the air. It flew directly to where the Baron, Matterhorn, and Bonehand were hiding in the grass. It folded its wings against its sleek body and screeched to earth like a smart bomb.

This was more than a natural predator guided by instinct. This hunter killed for sport and enjoyed delivering death with its talons. Screeching in fury, it aimed for Aaron's face.

The Baron and Matterhorn saw the danger at the same instant. They reacted to the attack as though their two bodies shared a single brain. As Aaron twisted hard right, Matterhorn drew his Sword and rolled into the vacant space.

A moment later the falcon skewered itself on Matterhorn's upraised blade.

The impact drove the hilt into Matterhorn's breastbone with a jarring crunch and knocked all the air from his lungs. Hot blood spurted over his trembling hands and chest. The extended talons tore his shirt and the open beak scratched his neck.

The Baron jumped up as the sound of shouting men came from below. The air attack was just the beginning of their troubles. "Get ready for more company!" he shouted.

Bonehand needed no encouragement. He straddled the crest of the hill, sword in hand. "There are only six men," he said over his shoulder. "How many do you want me to leave for you?"

Matterhorn crawled out from under the dead weight and stumbled to his feet, visibly shaken. "I, I've never killed anything bigger than a bug before," he stammered.

The Baron put a boot on the bird and pulled out the crimson shaft. He wiped the blade on the grass and handed the Sword to Matterhorn.

"I hate to see any animal killed," Bonehand said, "but that one deserved to die." He glanced down at the approaching pirates, armed to the teeth, and added, "It won't be the only blood spilt today."

The Baron rifled through Matterhorn's discarded pack and found two solar batteries from his security system. He tossed one to Matterhorn, and, a moment later, the toothbrush-sized sensor that went with it. "Set it up over there." He pointed to a spot and hurried to deploy an identical unit on the opposite side of the hill about twenty feet from the top.

Climbing back up, he said breathlessly, "Listen, Bonehand. No time to explain now, but when I say so, point your bony fingers at these guys and shout the scariest word you know at the top of your lungs.

"Get ready, here they come."

The pirates had reached the bottom of the knoll and started up. They snickered when they saw the three young men waiting at the top. These ruffians had brawled their way from the Mediterranean to the North Sea. They wore the scars of countless fights like badges of honor. Adept with knife and cutlass, they didn't expect much of a scuffle. All they wanted was to get rid of these meddlers, put the stinking animals on board ship, sail back to England, and collect their pay.

When the first two pirates reached the invisible line of electrons drawn by the Baron's sensors, he said to Bonehand, "Now!"

Bonehand threw back his cape and raised his right arm. He pointed a long, fleshless finger at the oncoming men and bellowed, "Fie!"

The thunder of Bonehand's deep voice was followed by a loud crackle of sideways lightning. The two men went down like moths flying into a bug-zapper. Their limbs twitched as they lay smoldering on the ground. Smoke leaked out from under their bandanas and the stench of burnt hair wafted up the hill.

The remaining pirates froze in mid-stride.

"What in blazes was that?" Bonehand staggered back and stared at his index finger.

"Would you believe sorcery?"

"I don't believe in sorcery."

"How about magic, then?"

"Don't believe in that either."

"If you must know," the Baron said, "it's called electricity. It will be very popular one day. But don't tell anyone you heard about it from me."

Still bewildered, Bonehand asked, "Are those men dead?"

"No. But they won't be any more bother to us." Then the Baron scowled at Bonehand and said, "What kind of scary word is 'fie'? Is that the best you can do?"

Before Bonehand could respond, the Baron nodded toward the rest of their attackers. "Get ready to point again. I bet you can scare these boys back to the beach."

He was right. As soon as Bonehand aimed his finger, the pirates left their smoking buddies and ran away at the speed of fear.

The captain had been watching from the corral when the two men had gone down in a crackling blue flash. A few moments later, he saw the rest of the band beat a hasty retreat. He was too far away to tell what had happened, but he knew how to counter it. Cupping his hands to his mouth, he bellowed to his ship, "Unfriendlies on the hill! Open fire!"

The command carried easily across open water, and the first mate put his spyglass to his eye. He quickly spotted the three locals on the grassy knoll. Since the eight shore-side canons were kept primed and loaded, the first volley was on its way within a minute.

"Incoming!" the Baron yelled. The warning was unnecessary as Matterhorn and Bonehand were already scrambling into the woods behind the hill. The lead balls punched great holes in the earth and threw up geysers of dirt, but since they didn't contain explosives, they posed little threat to the men now hidden in the trees.

The captain soon realized this and yelled to his crew, "Cease fire! All hands to shore! Make it quick!"

The deck burst into activity as the first mate barked orders. This was his maiden voyage with this crew, but they had quickly learned the captain was not a man to cross. He had tossed two men overboard for nothing more than spilling a keg of rum. He had run the navigator through with his cutlass for a slight error that cost them time in reaching Ireland.

Several sailors scrambled down a cargo net into dinghies that bounced against the wooden hull. They filled the boats to overflowing and strong arms were soon pulling the oars with practiced precision.

The eager crew should have reached the captain in a few minutes—but they never got near the beach.

Water Nymph

AS the pirates hurried to obey the shore call, they rowed into unexpected difficulty. Despite the calm day, the water around them bunched into waves and resisted their efforts. Like a riptide, the reverse current pushed them away from land. Three-foot waves became six-foot breakers, then doubled again to twelve-foot monsters! The ocean rose so rapidly that even the most veteran seadogs among them had never seen anything like it. Terror melted their bones and bleached their faces.

The rogue waves not only toyed with the pirates, they easily lifted the schooner and tossed it toward the horizon. The swells had grown so huge that the ship's anchor was useless.

Nothing but panicky screams made it to land. The captain fumed and cursed at his lost ship. He couldn't care less about the men, but this supernatural interference might pose a real problem.

Karn was also upset, but for a different reason. Coming down the beach toward him were the three men in the world he *never* wanted to see again. He jerked the captain's sleeve and frantically pointed at the oncoming figures. "Don't let them get near me," Karn pleaded. "I'll give you anything you want."

The captain backhanded Karn off the rail. "I'll *take* anything I want, you sniveling shrimp," he growled.

True, he needed the leprechaun to carry the Flute back to England. But that would be difficult now that his ship was gone. He would have to use the raft until he could steal something better.

First things first. These intruders had to be killed. The captain marshaled his remaining crew. Leaving two men by the animals, he drew his cutlass and led the charge.

Matterhorn, the Baron, and Bonehand marched toward the pirates. The trio had decided to go on the offensive, ignoring the fact that they were outnumbered. They were as startled as the pirates by what had just happened out on the bay. But at least Matterhorn and the Baron knew what had caused it. Or, more precisely, whom.

"The water nymph must have followed us," Matterhorn exclaimed as he stared after the receding boats. "She can do incredible things with water!"

Bonehand scowled. "We still have plenty to worry about here on land. These knaves aren't as squeamish about spilling blood as you, Matterhorn. They'll cut us into fish bait." He looked at the Baron and asked, "You got any more tricks in your bag?"

"I'm glad you asked." The Baron produced an eight-inch aluminum tube, unfolded two hinged arms, unscrewed the bottom and removed a heavy rubber band. His nimble fingers moved over the tube, transforming it into a magnum slingshot. Without breaking stride he scooped up a few golf-ball-sized rocks and opened fire.

The first stone flew over the pirates' heads. They taunted the Baron for his lousy aim.

The heckling stopped when the next rock laid the second mate out like a clubbed seal. He got off a few more rounds before running out of ammo on the sandy beach. He folded the weapon away and pulled a mahogany handle from a pencil-thin sleeve on his other leg.

Bonehand marveled. "Now what?"

"This is what I prefer for close-in fighting," Aaron replied. He pressed a button on the stick and released an eight-foot lash with a polished metal tip. "I call it a switch-whip. Made it myself."

"That's the best you can do for weapons?" Matterhorn cried. "Slingshots and bullwhips!" He was hoping for laser guns and hand grenades!

The Baron patted his pockets and said, "I've got a few throwing stars somewhere. Don't worry, I can hold my own. How about you? Afraid?"

"Terrified!"

"Just hold tight to that Sword," the Baron said, "You'll be okay."

The blade pulsed and Matterhorn felt the handle throb in sync. The power is in the Maker's Sword, he reminded himself. He was just the delivery boy. No, make that man. He was taller than any of the oncoming sailors and certainly better armed. Perhaps he *could* hold his own in a fight. Hadn't he and the Sword just saved the Baron's life? He looked down at his sticky hands and the stained silver crosspiece, evidence of their baptism in blood.

The captain who had sent the gyrfalcon would show no mercy to Broc or the other animals in the corral. The thought of what would happen to them if this rescue attempt failed doubled Matterhorn's determination. Karn's treachery and the captain's cruelty could not go unpunished.

The faster his mind churned, the faster his feet moved and soon Matterhorn was several paces ahead of the Baron and Bonehand, zeroing in on the captain like a heat-seeking bomb.

The pirate watched the youth's charge and realized the young fool knew nothing about staying alive in a fight. He had committed himself too soon; narrowed his focus too early. The captain hand signaled two men into ambush position. Under his breath he snarled, "Let's grant this idiot his death wish."

Matterhorn was so focused on the captain that he never saw the men with the net until they blindsided him. The unexpected blow knocked the Sword from his hand and trapped him like a tuna, arms pinned helplessly by his sides. The air was crushed out of his lungs by the two goons on his back. Their sweaty bulk smashed him into the sand and squeezed bile up into his throat. His muscles quivered beneath the terrible weight. His heart jack-hammered against his bruised ribs.

All the bravery left his body along with his breath.

Thoughts of Broc and the Flute disappeared, replaced by images of the family he would never see again. They were hundreds of years in the future and thousands of miles away in a place where he himself had been only a few days ago. A safe place.

A place he should never have left!

Beach Brawl

BONEHAND and the Baron had no chance to help Matterhorn before they came under attack themselves. Four men circled Bonehand, blades carving the air. He parried their flashing steel with his short sword. "You fight like women!" he taunted. "Be thankful I'm not using my good hand!" He raised his skeletal right hand and rattled the bones.

Two sailors drew back in horror, but a third saw his chance and darted in under the uplifted arm. Expecting the attack, Bonehand deftly swirled his cape around the man's sword and jerked it from his grasp. Then he followed up with a side kick to the groin. He feigned to the left with his sword; then leapt to the right and flung the cape over a pirate's head. Yanking his victim forward, he brought his knee up into the man's stomach and the pommel of his sword down on the man's head.

As he spun to face his remaining assailants, Bonehand did not see a fifth man move in from behind. A seasoned brawler, he stayed out of harm's way. He picked up a rock and waited.

The men in front of Bonehand charged. Occupied with this onslaught, Bonehand did not see the rock. Because of that, he did not see anything else for a long time.

Meanwhile, the Baron had troubles of his own. Several pirates tried to get close enough to use their cutlasses on him, but his snarling whip kept them at bay. One man received a deep cut on his arm for his boldness. The Baron counted silently—one, two, three— until the smitten sailor slid to the sand, conscious yet unmoving.

The tip of the lash was coated with a mild form of the poison, curare. The Baron had learned that little paralyzing trick from Nate.

The whip wasn't Aaron's only weapon. A flick of his wrist zipped a throwing star into the forearm of a burly man, who dropped his cutlass and cursed in pain. He twisted away just in time to keep a second star from giving him a close shave.

With calm precision the Baron stunned a second pirate, then a third, with his lash. But more kept coming as those who had knocked out Bonehand came over. Everyone at the beach brawl now clustered around Aaron, except the captain and the two men on top of Matterhorn.

In desperation he whirled the whip overhead like a helicopter blade to create a no-man's-land around him. But that could only last until his arm gave out.

Nearby, Matterhorn's world shifted into slow motion and a single thought bounced around in his head: I'm gonna die! I'm gonna die! I'm gonna DIE!

"No," interrupted a calm voice. "That is not why you are here."

The voice in his head startled Matterhorn more than what was happening to his body.

"You have a job to do," the voice continued. "The only way you can fail is if you quit. I have given you all the power you need."

Who had given him what power? The only thing he had with any power was the Sword, and now even that was gone.

"The Sword is just one of my tools," the voice said. "I can work without it, and so can you. Use what you have. It is enough."

I don't belong here, Matterhorn silently protested. This is all a big mistake. I'm not a knight; I'm just a kid!

"You are what I have called you to be."

Matterhorn lay at a crossroads. He could give in to his circumstances or rise up to his calling. He had been given an adult body; did he have the courage to use it? He had just been told he wasn't meant to die here; did he believe it? He didn't have to be a victim; he could be a victor.

Victor!

That's it!

Matterhorn had learned some great wrestling moves from his older brother Victor, and now he had the body mass to use them to full effect! But would his new muscles remember what his twelve-year-old muscles knew? Only one way to find out.

When one of the attackers shifted to the side to get at his knife, Matterhorn erupted. Despite the net, he raised his head and upper body and did an adrenalin-powered post-and-roll. He got up on his right elbow while curling his leg around the other pirate's left knee. Then he twisted his bulk the opposite direction and flipped the startled man over like a turtle.

He followed this with an illegal forearm chop across the throat. The blow would keep the man from thinking about anything but breathing for a while.

The other brute had his knife out by now. He lunged forward and stabbed at Matterhorn's stomach. But Matterhorn's knee was already coming up to deflect the murderous blow. Still, the blade cut through his pants and sliced his thigh. Through the pain he forced his leg farther upward; then brought his heel down hard into the man's kidney. This straightened the pirate upright in agony. Matterhorn did a power sit-up and head-butted the brute, putting his lights out.

Untangling himself, Matterhorn scurried across the sand like a crab and scooped up the Sword. His ribs ached from a second bruising. His leg throbbed from the stab wound. He ignored the pain as he checked the battle scene.

Bonehand lay unmoving amidst several downed pirates.

The Baron was fighting for his life in the center of a tightening ring of flashing steel.

The captain waited nearby, letting his men do the dirty work.

When Matterhorn locked eyes with him, the captain jeered. "You handle yourself pretty well. Let's see how you handle this!"

Mortal Combat

THE captain came forward, cutlass first. Matterhorn raised his Sword to deflect the expected blow. His attacker froze, gaze fixed on the blade, which now glowed like a beam of sunlight. The brilliance cast a shadow of fear on the captain's face and he weighed his chances in this new light. More than anyone else on the beach, he understood the incredible power of that Sword. But did the young man know what he held?

Matterhorn took advantage of the pause to slow his breathing and his heart rate. The anger in his chest cooled from hot flames to embers. A peace settled over him as he recalled the Baron's words from their first meeting: "You're safer with this Sword in your hands than if you were inside a tank." And hadn't he just been told that the only way he could fail was if he quit?

He shook the sweat from his forehead and read the indecision on the captain's face. This raised his confidence. He felt like a fighter pilot at the controls of an awesome weapon. Only a fool would challenge the Maker's Sword in combat.

The captain was no fool. The blade's light and Matterhorn's body language told him he had no chance. The shadow of fear gave way to the thing itself. He drew back from a fight he could not win and dare not start. Yes, the others would be furious with his failure to get the Flute. But if he stayed alive, he could try again later.

The captain took another step backward. Then another.

With amazing speed the Sword pulled Matterhorn toward the retreating pirate, and in a crash of blades the battle began!

Matterhorn had all he could do to hold onto the Sword. The captain had all he could do to block the blows. He knew he had to get the Sword out of Matterhorn's hands if he wanted to survive. And the best way to do that was to go low.

When Matterhorn swung his next roundhouse, the captain met it with his cutlass. But rather than resist the blow, he let it knock him backwards and down. Like a judo master using an opponent's strength to gain the advantage, he rolled and brought his legs forward to sweep Matterhorn's feet from under him.

Matterhorn landed hard and the air whooshed from his lungs in one great UUGGHH! His head smacked a piece of driftwood and everything went out of focus. The Sword lay in his limp hand. He didn't have the strength to grip it, much less lift it.

The captain jumped up and should have run. But seeing Matterhorn down and dazed, a murderous urge came over him. He lunged in for the quick kill.

Not quick enough.

A jolt of power shot from the hilt of the Sword, up Matterhorn's arm and into his chest. His body jerked as though being shocked back to life from a heart attack. His arm came up and the Sword of Truth sliced the captain's cutlass in half as if it was a stick.

It was Matterhorn's turn to use his legs to down his attacker. The captain landed on his back and Matterhorn leapt to his feet. Just that quick, their roles were reversed and Matterhorn held his Sword point an inch above the pirate's chest.

The man's unblinking eyes were pure evil. His voice dripped with contempt as he snarled, "You wouldn't kill an unarmed man. You don't have it in you."

Matterhorn knew the pirate was right, yet a moment later he stared horrified as the Sword—under its own power—plunged into the captain's chest to the hilt.

Instead of blood pouring from the wound, a foul-smelling mist spewed upward. The body dissolved into a thick black stench and hissed off the blade in sooty steam leaving a pile of empty clothes in the sand.

What had he done?

What had the Sword done?

Maybe the Baron could tell him.

The Baron!

The thought jerked Matterhorn out of his stupor and spun him around. "Aaron! Are you okay?"

"I could use some help here!" came a loud yell.

Matterhorn started toward where his friend stood entrapped by attackers. The two guards from the corral had grown impatient and run up the beach to join the skirmish. That put the number of men surrounding Aaron at six.

Adrenaline still pumped through his veins, but Matterhorn was having trouble putting weight on his wounded leg. It would take him a minute to get to his friend.

"You seem to be doing fine!" he shouted as he limped forward. "I'd hate to interrupt!"

"Interrupt! Interrupt!" the Baron cried. "My arm's about to fall off."

Matterhorn feared he wouldn't make it to his partner in time. Suddenly, the flash of an idea lit up his brain. He stopped and yelled to the Baron, "Hang on, buddy! I salute your bravery!" He gave a mock salute; then pivoted his hand down to shield his eyes.

Would the Baron understand?

Aaron saw the hand motion and picked up the signal. He thought he knew what Matterhorn wanted him to do. In an act of supreme trust he dropped his whip and covered his eyes with both hands.

If he had guessed wrong, he was dead.

End Game

MATTERHORN put his fingers to his lips and whistled as loud as he could. The pirates turned at the unexpected sound—and were blinded by a dazzling flash from the Sword. Matterhorn felt the heat surge on the forearm that shielded his face. When he opened his eyes, everyone but the Baron was blind as a barnacle.

"That's some brilliant Swordplay," the Baron said with great relief. "I'm glad we're on the same side."

"That makes two of us," Matterhorn panted. He hobbled forward, using the Sword for a cane.

"Keep an eye on these goons while I get my pack," Aaron said. "I have some rope we can put to good use."

Back at the corral, Karn had cowered behind a post and waited for a chance to escape. When the guards left to join the fight, he took off in the opposite direction as fast as his stubby legs would go. He covered a half-mile of open sand before turning up the nearest stream. He waded in the middle of the water to hide his trail.

Karn splashed upriver like a salmon going to spawn. It frightened him to be in the water since he didn't know how to swim. But he was even more terrified of being caught. Whoever won the fight would come after the Flute—and his head!

His new plan was simple: get to his hidden boat and wait for darkness. Then sneak back to the bay and out to sea. The current would carry him down-coast to a fishing village he knew. He would hide there until he could catch a ship—any ship—away from the captain's wrath and the strangers' revenge.

Grasping the pouch of gold that had been the down payment for the Flute, Karn pushed onward. It was only half of what the captain had promised, but it would buy Karn a fresh start. He would never have to mend shoes or tend shop again. And he still had the Flute. He could sell it again wherever he went. Just a few more hours of luck, and he would be on his way to the life he deserved.

When Karn reached the hills, the stream widened and flowed more swiftly. He stayed in the shallows, but he slipped and fell several times on the slimy rocks. At last, he saw his skiff where he'd tied it to an overhanging branch. Just a few more yards.

But when the leprechaun turned toward shore, the current grabbed his legs and sent him cartwheeling into deeper water. He was dunked, flipped, spun, tumbled, whirled, and would have drowned if not for the woman who suddenly appeared and carried his almost lifeless body to a sandbar in midstream.

The turbulent water should keep Karn from escaping when he came to his senses. The woman took the Flute from around his neck and dissolved into a wave to carry it back to the bay.

The animals in the corral awoke from their dream-state at that precise moment. As long as Karn had the Flute, and played it regularly, they remained under his spell. But once the Flute and the player were separated, the enchantment dissolved. The songbirds flew to safety while the squirrels and foxes tried to avoid being trampled by the larger animals.

Broc kicked down the makeshift gate and headed toward Matterhorn. The unicorn followed, trailing a tail of foxes. The horse and rider shared a joyous reunion, standing cheek-to-cheek for a long time; each thankful the other was all right. They had grown so close over these past danger-filled days that words were unnecessary.

Nearby, the Baron tended to Bonehand, using smelling salts to revive him.

"I wasn't much help," Bonehand rasped. "I feel like I've been kicked by a mule." Several of the animals gathered around, licking his face and hands. He smiled and winced at the same time. It was worth the splitting headache to know they were safe.

"You did fine," the Baron said, handing Bonehand two aspirin. "Don't ask what these are; just swallow them."

After taking the pills, Bonehand began picking sand from the honey that coated his wrist. "This is why I don't like the beach," he mumbled.

Aaron walked over and removed his belt from Broc's neck. "Glad you're okay." He turned to Matterhorn and said, "You, not so okay. Let's get a look at your leg."

Matterhorn sat down and rested the Sword across his lap. His hands were shaking. "Have you ever killed anyone before?" he asked the Baron.

"No," Aaron replied as he knelt to inspect Matterhorn's wound. "And I don't intend to. That's why I carry a whip and not a sword." He cut the torn pant leg off above the knee. "You haven't killed anybody either," he assured Matterhorn. "That thing wasn't human."

Matterhorn winced at the Baron's probing. "He seemed human enough—until the Sword pierced him."

"The cut isn't too deep," the Baron said as he cleaned sand from the gash with an alcohol swab.

Matterhorn gripped the Sword hilt with both hands to keep from screaming.

"Put that Sword down and pinch the flaps of skin together," the Baron ordered. "No, like this." From a white tube, he squeezed a bead of clear paste on the laceration.

"What's that?" Matterhorn wanted to know.

"Super glue. It works better than stitches, and it won't leave a scar."

"Do you read this stuff in books or make it up as you go along?" Matterhorn said, amazed at the range of Aaron's knowledge and skill.

The Baron grinned. "I can't answer that or you might sue me for malpractice."

"Well, I appreciate it," Matterhorn said. He borrowed the Baron's knife and sliced off his other pant leg to match.

"And I appreciate you," Aaron said as he put away his first-aid kit. "Thanks for saving my life."

"You're welcome," Matterhorn replied.

"And mine, too," said a voice that sounded like Queen Bea.

But when Matterhorn looked up, all he saw was the unicorn.

Lost and Found

"IS-IS that you, Your Highness?" the Baron sputtered. He stood and approached the unicorn.

"Do you like my disguise? Unicorns are one of my favorite animals."

The creature's lips never moved, but Matterhorn heard the words in his mind. Now he remembered what the horn reminded him of: the opals in Queen Bea's throne and crown.

Just then, a luminous glittering began at the tip of the unicorn's horn, transforming it into a sparkling fuse. The horn melted and flattened into a gold-and-opal coronet. The long mane spun into tresses of brown hair. Four feet became two. Open-toed sandals replaced hooves. The face shortened; the body lengthened as the regal animal morphed into a royal lady.

Queen Bea stood on the beach dressed in a charcoal gray traveling outfit. On her left wrist she wore a lion-headed charm bracelet from which dangled several beautifully carved miniature animals: an ivory eagle, a coral dolphin, a jade dragon, a gold tiger, and a granite mouse. She transferred a tiny opal unicorn from her palm to the bracelet.

The Baron was more upset than happy at the sudden revelation. "You took a terrible risk coming here," he scolded in an older-brother tone. "You could have been injured or killed."

"I am not helpless," Bea shot back. "And I am *not* in the habit of asking for permission to do what I see fit."

Before the Baron could continue the argument, the two men who had been zapped on the hill staggered into view. They offered no resistance and were quickly tied up with the rest of the pirates at the corral. The men weren't so mean now that their captain was gone.

The interruption gave the Queen time to get over her pique. When the Baron and Matterhorn rejoined her, she said, "I came to Ireland and assumed this form so I would hear the Flute if it was played. I thought I would be able to resist its spell, resume my natural form, and recover the Talis." Her gaze dropped to the sand and she added, "I was wrong. The wonderful music completely overwhelmed me. My whole being surrendered to pure joy. I would gladly have followed Karn anywhere, done anything he asked."

"Speaking of the Flute," the Baron said, pointing to a large red fox trotting toward them with the silver tube in his mouth. This animal hadn't gone with the others after being freed from the corral, but had picked up Karn's trail instead. He tracked the leprechaun to the

stream. He didn't have to go any farther because he saw
the Flute gliding on top of the water. He paddled in and
scooped up the instrument, still attached to its necklace,
and brought it to the Queen.

"The Maker be praised!" Bea cried, as she knelt to
grasp the necklace and put it around her neck. "You
have done well," she said, touching the fox with the tip
of the Flute. A shimmering spread over the sleek body,
darkening the rusty fur to black—all but the tips of the
hair, which lightened to silver. "Receive this new coat as
a token of my gratitude."

"I thought Travelers weren't supposed to interfere
with the natural order of things?" the Baron said as Bea
stood.

"Will you find fault with everything I do? There is no
harm in rewarding this clever fellow with a bright new
outfit."

The fox pranced over to show off his new colors to
Bonehand, who had been watching the proceedings with
a growing sense of wonder. The unicorn queen's beauty
and power left him breathless.

Bea followed the fox and offered Bonehand a hand
up. She waved off his normal left hand and accepted his
skeletal right without flinching. "I have heard of your
love for animals and of your bravery," she said as he
rose. "I have seen both today. The fox has his recom-
pense; how may I reward you?"

After a long silence, Bonehand said, "You came for
the Flute. If you take it with you when you go, that is
enough."

Bea nodded and smiled. "I must explain this to King Ian in person. Will you help me find him?"

"Happily," Bonehand said. "Just as soon as I make sure the animals are all right."

"No hurry," Bea replied. "I have other matters to attend myself." With that she herded the Baron and Matterhorn up the beach for a private conversation.

Matterhorn felt great as he walked between the Baron and the Queen. Broc and the other animals were safe. The Flute had been recovered. Maybe he could go home now. But first he had a few questions. "Pardon me, Your Majesty," he said. "The pirate captain I fought; who was he? What was he?"

"He was a wraith from First Realm," the Queen said. "And I owe you an apology. If I had known you would encounter a dark spirit on your first trip, I would never have sent you. His presence here is deeply troubling."

"How did a wraith get to Ireland?" the Baron asked.

"The heretics somehow discovered the Flute's whereabouts and sent him for it. He used the guise of a pirate captain to get a crew and a ship to bring him from the portal in England. Fortunately he did not have the Traveler's Cube or he could have come and gone before we had a chance to stop him."

"Heretics?" Matterhorn said in a one-word question.

The Queen fixed her large brown eyes on Matterhorn. "Even in the Realm there are those who reject the Maker's way," she said. "They ignore the sacred doctrine of noninterference and want to control the destinies of others. These heretics desire the Talis for evil purposes.

Their agent, the wraith, learned of Karn and his resentment toward Ian. He put the knowledge to good use, promising Karn a great sum for the Flute."

"The greedy little leprechaun," Aaron muttered.

"All was going according to plan until you two arrived," Bea continued. "Karn tried everything to get rid of you. He made the bone bomb. He hired the kidnappers. He even torched the mill at his trading post."

"How do you know all this?" Matterhorn asked.

"I have been keeping an eye on you," the Queen replied. "For a couple of *secret* agents, you sure attracted a lot of attention."

"It's not our fault," Aaron protested.

"Now what?" Matterhorn wanted to know.

"Karn must pay for his crimes," Bea said. "Bonehand and I will find the scoundrel and take him with us to see Ian. The king can decide how to deal with his nephew. And as a Queen," she added in a regal tone, "I know how to deal with you."

Knight Time

THE trio had reached a secluded inlet and the Queen turned to her rescuers. "Kneel before me," she commanded.

Matterhorn and the Baron exchanged puzzled looks and then did as ordered.

She stepped up to Aaron first and said, "You have served well on many assignments and shown surprising skill with the Traveler's Cube. The Praetorians were right about you. For this, as well as your cleverness and courage, I grant you in the Maker's name the honor of keeping the Cube. You may come and go as you please. No other Traveler has ever been given such freedom. Use it wisely."

Ever since his first trip with the Cube, Aaron had devoted himself to learning its intricacies. Now he could take it to the next level. "Thank you, Your Majesty," he said.

"As for you," Bea said, shifting her attention to Matterhorn. "When we first met, I sensed you had great potential. The Sword would not have called you other-wise. Still, one never knows if a person will become all he or she can be, or stay who they are. You have grown from an untested youth into a knight. Give me the Sword."

Matterhorn drew the hilt, extended the blade, and handed the Talis to the Queen.

Dubbing him on both shoulders, she pronounced, "For bravery in serving me and the Maker, I grant you in His name the rank of Queen's Knight. Henceforth you will be known as Matterhorn the Brave."

"I don't deserve the honor," Matterhorn protested. "I've been more scared than brave these last few days."

"It is not true bravery unless you are truly afraid," Bea said.

Aaron the Baron nudged Matterhorn. "That's one for your little book."

As he stood, Matterhorn thought of all that had hap-pened since he'd been pulled into the Propylon and sent to Ireland. He saw a swirl of faces: Aaron, Ian, Bonehand, Broc, Karn, the captain. He recalled the faceless voice that had said, *"I have called you a knight."* And now he was one!

He had been chosen.

He had been called.

He had obeyed.

There was only one thing he hadn't done.

"Your Majesty?"

"Yes?"

"May I hold the Flute?"

Bea smiled as she laid the ten-inch silver shaft in his palms. It was more like a miniature recorder than a modern flute, Matterhorn noticed. It had no valves, just six finger holes and a thumbhole. It felt cool to the touch and heavier than he expected. He sensed both the lilt of a morning sunrise and the bass of an afternoon thunderstorm in its short span. A deep joy bubbled in his heart as he ran his fingers over the words inscribed in flowing script: *Play with joy in creation's symphony.*

"This is the Talis of the Maker's joy," Bea explained as Aaron the Baron took a turn with the sacred instrument. "The Chief Musician of the Realm plays it on special occasions to celebrate the joy of creation. Now she will be able to do so once more."

As the Queen put the Flute back around her neck, there came a loud splash from behind her. She turned toward the sea and said, "There is someone else I need to reward." Presently the spray above the rocks formed into the shapely lady from Karn's mill.

The Queen made the introductions. "Aaron the Baron, Matterhorn the Brave, this is Sara." The water naiad and the unicorn had met on the Queen's first day in the country and Sara had agreed to help protect the Travelers.

"We met a few nights ago," Aaron said. "She got us out of a real hot spot."

"That was a neat trick getting rid of the schooner and her crew today," Matterhorn added.

"Thank you," Sara replied with a twinkle in her voice that matched the sparkle in her eyes. Her delicate features were unchanged, but today she wore an ocean blue gossamer frock accented by a purple amethyst necklace and earrings. Her nail polish had deepened to purple.

"Your help has been invaluable," Bea said. "What can I do to show my appreciation?"

"Ireland is lovely," Sara said, "yet there's so much more to see and experience of the Maker's creation. Let me travel in your service. You have seen what I can do." Lowering her voice, she added, "These men are strong and resourceful; still, they could use a lady's help from time to time."

Bea smiled. "So they could."

"Now wait a minute!" the Baron spoke up. "We don't travel all the time. And when we do, it's dangerous."

"All the more reason I should come along," Sara said coyly.

"I think it's a bad idea," Aaron grumbled.

"And I think it is a good one," the Queen announced. "Request granted. Baron, what sort of containers do you have in those pockets of yours?"

"He's got a vial of smelling salts," Matterhorn offered, for which he earned a scowl.

"That will do. Empty it."

The Baron did so and scrubbed out the ammonia smell with sand and salt water. The plastic tube with its rubber stopper was about as long as his little finger. "This is awfully tiny," he said. "I don't know what good this will do."

"It is sufficient for me," Sara said.

"What?" You're going to live in this?"

"It will hold my essence," Sara explained. "Whenever you open the vial, I can make a body and clothes to suit me out of any nearby water."

"Won't you be lonely in the meantime?" Matterhorn asked.

The nymph shook her head. "I don't experience time except when I'm in a body. My next thought will be when I take shape again. I can't wait to see where that will be!"

"Before you go, Sara," Bea said, "would you mind returning the pirate ship? We have some beached sailors who need a ride home."

"I only pushed it a few miles away," Sara said. "The evening tide will bring it back. And now, by your leave." She bowed and then dissolved into a fine mist that condensed into the vial. Her gems plunked into the sand at the Baron's feet.

Aaron capped the tube, feeling uneasy about the arrangement; yet secretly glad he would see Sara again.

Fond Farewell

THUS began the good-byes. When Bea and the Travelers rejoined Bonehand and the others, Matterhorn's spirits sank. Everyone he'd met in Ireland would be long dead when he returned to his own time. He would never get to ride Broc again. He would never know if Bonehand and Ian patched up their differences. Still, the prospect of going home helped to offset the sadness.

The Baron, who wrestled with the same mixed emotions, was first to speak. "We have to be going now," he told Bonehand. "We couldn't have found the Flute without you. Thanks for your help."

"You saved my life," Bonehand said. "Let's call it even." He held out his hand and both the Baron and Matterhorn shook it without reservation. The grip was firm even though the fingers felt like a bundle of sticks. "You are welcome in my woods any time."

"Probably won't happen," the Baron replied. "We live a long way from here."

Broc pushed his way amongst the humans. Matterhorn pulled a squished Snickers from his pocket. He had been saving it for the post-rescue party. He rubbed Broc's birthmark while the horse ate the treat.

"I know you're a free creature and you go where you want," Matterhorn whispered. "Still, you might check on Bonehand once in a while. He's got a lot of territory to watch over; he could sure use your help."

Matterhorn hardly needed to mention this. Bonehand's respect for the horse's intelligence and the care he had taken for Broc's wound had started a friendship that would last a lifetime.

Aaron tapped Matterhorn on the shoulder. "We should be on our way. With your permission," he said to the Queen.

"Granted. Walk with the Maker."

"Always."

"That's it?" Matterhorn said, staring at Bea. "We just stroll into the sunset?"

Bea smiled. "Only if you can walk on water like Sara."

"It's a figure of speech. But seriously, we just leave?"

"I will see to the final details. You are free to go. Do not look so worried my brave knight," Bea added. "Remember what I told you when we first met—serve well, serve long. You will be summoned again."

The Baron and Matterhorn left the crowd at the corral and started along the beach. They took time to find all the Baron's throwing stars. They would leave no evidence of their presence behind except their prints in the shifting sands of memory.

On the climb up the knoll to retrieve their packs, the Baron asked, "How did you manage that great escape from the goons with the net?"

"Have you ever heard the Maker's voice?"

With a knowing smile Aaron said, "What you can become . . ."

". . . you already are," Matterhorn completed the sentence. He stopped on the spot and wrote the phrase on the first page of his quote book.

Once atop the hill, Aaron collected his electric eyes while Matterhorn stared at the bloody gyrfalcon, its beak open and its talons empty in death. That had been a close call. He thought of the Sword that had saved his life. Already he missed the weight of it on his hip, the feel of the soft leather in his palm, the brilliant hardness of the blade.

"Change your clothes," the Baron said, handing Matterhorn his pack. "Put everything in here. Then I'll take you home."

"It's pretty cool that the Queen let you keep the Traveler's Cube," Matterhorn said while switching shirts.

"It's a great honor," the Baron said. "And so is being called by the Sword of Truth. It makes you a Traveler."

Matterhorn knelt to tie his shoes. "What exactly do Travelers do?"

"First Realm opens portals on other worlds and monitors the civilizations there," the Baron explained. "If they mature to where all the cultures are living in harmony, the Realm makes contact and invites them into the Alliance."

"You mean like a United Nations of the universe?"

"Sort of," the Baron replied. "When Praetorians from the Realm set up the portals, they select and train locals to become Travelers. They are recruited as kids and retired when their bodies can no longer handle the strain of time jumping—usually in their twenties. Travelers gather information and make progress reports."

"How many portals are there on Earth?" Matterhorn asked.

"About two dozen that I know of, probably more. Some are in well-known places like the Great Pyramid in Egypt and near Stonehenge."

"The rock formation in England?"

"Yeah," the Baron said. "That's how both the Queen and the wraith got here."

Aaron ran his fingers through his short-cropped hair and put on his red baseball cap. "Everything changed not long ago because of the trouble in First Realm," he went on. "I'm sure that has something to do with me getting to keep the Cube." He put the Talis in his pack.

"Don't you need that to take me home?" Matterhorn asked.

"I don't know your time-space coordinates," Aaron said as he pulled out the hilt of the Sword of Truth. The Queen had given it to him for just this purpose. "You're returning the way you came." The diamond blade extended and he stuck it in the ground. Then he rested his left hand on Matterhorn's shoulder in the Traveler's salute.

Matterhorn returned the gesture of respect and said, "I'm going to miss you, Aaron. As Ashleigh Brilliant once wrote, 'We've been through so much together, and most of it was your fault.'"

The Baron responded with a quote of his own. "Methinks the gentleman doth protest too much." He stepped back a few paces and said, "Put your hands on the hilt."

Matterhorn widened his stance and did so.

"Serve well, my friend . . ."

". . . serve long," Matterhorn finished.

The ground beneath him dissolved and as he stretched into nothingness, he heard the Baron say, "Try to land on your feet this time."

Lucky Charm

THE ringing in his ears persisted. Matt tried to lift his head, but a swirl of dizziness kept him facedown. When the noise died away, he gradually realized it had been a bell. Opening his eyes, he found himself back in the library at David R. Sanford Middle School. The clock above Miss Tull's desk read 3:01.

Impossible!

He'd been traveling for days, yet the clock had ticked off only a few minutes.

Matt sat up and rubbed the bump on his forehead. He must have dozed off and smacked his head on the desk. There was something large in his lap. An open book. He flipped it over and read the title printed on the spine.

The Sword and the Flute.

The book was much lighter than when he had pulled it off Mr. Rickets. The pages were filled with words, whereas before they had been blank. The hole in the middle was gone.

As he skimmed the story, Matt realized he had just lived it. He read of the Propylon and Queen Bea. Of Aaron the Baron and the Sword of Truth. He flipped ahead to Ireland. Ian, the king of the leprechauns was described just as Matt remembered him. So were Broc and Bonehand.

Matt slammed the book shut and closed his eyes.

He could feel the Baron's hand on his shoulder in a Traveler's salute.

He could sense the Sword of Truth pulsing in his palm.

He could recall the texture of Broc's birthmark.

He could remember Bonehand's skeletal grip.

He could taste burnt caterpillar.

He could hear the Maker's voice. *"What you can become you already are."*

Another voice was speaking to him now.

"Are you all right, Matt?" Miss Tull asked. "What happened?" She touched the bruise on his forehead.

"I'm okay," Matt said. "I must have fallen asleep and bumped my head." He got up a little shakily and walked over to Mr. Rickets to return the book. As he slid it in place, the gold lettering on the spine faded. The disappearing act made his vision swim. He stumbled backwards and rubbed his eyes.

"I'd better take you to see the nurse," Miss Tull said, coming toward him.

"I'm fine, really." Matt hurried away before she could grab his forearm and steer him to Mrs. Serveen. Mrs.

Serveen had been the school nurse since the days of Florence Nightingale. She had the bedside manner of a drill sergeant. No kid ever went to her of his own free will.

Matt's first stop when he left the library was the boy's bathroom. After he examined the bruise on his forehead, he checked his right leg. There was no sign of a knife wound. And when he peeked down his shirt, he found no bruises on his chest. His ribs felt fine.

His ponytail was gone, too, he noticed sadly. His twelve-year-old body looked small and feeble. Had he really been an adult only a few minutes ago?

The halls were almost deserted by the time Matt reached his locker, this being Friday afternoon. He walked out to where his sister usually met him, but she was gone. Probably got tired of waiting and went home alone. That was okay. Matt needed time to think.

Trudging past the park, he waved off his friends who were kicking a soccer ball around. "See you tomorrow!" one of them yelled. "We're gonna be champs!"

So he hadn't missed the district championships. He hadn't been gone for days. His overactive imagination had simply created a far-out story. Clocks don't lie, he scolded himself. Neither do mirrors. Still, something scratched at the back of his mind that wouldn't let him dismiss his adventure as a daydream.

The scratching turned out to be on his left wrist. Matt noticed it as he swung his arms in stride. When he finally realized what it was, a slow smile spread across his freckled face and a deep joy settled in his heart.

He *had* been to First Realm and back.

He *had* fought in Ireland alongside the Baron and been knighted by the Queen.

The Sword and the Flute were not figments of his imagination. They were Talis from another world.

He was a Traveler now.

All the proof he needed was right there on his belt. And the rest of the way home he couldn't stop rubbing his new lucky charm.

A scritch pad.

Epilogue

THE Monday after Matthew Horn returned from Ireland, he arrived at school by 6:30 a.m. When the custodian unlocked the doors, Matt mumbled something about an unfinished assignment and begged to be let into the library. Once there, he headed straight for Mr. Rickets. With shaking hands, Matt pulled out *The Sword and the Flute*. He sat on the floor and speed-read it once more.

How these words got into the once-blank book wasn't the only question on Matt's mind. He wanted to know if there were other stories among Mr. Ricket's treasures that had "holes" in them. Carefully at first, then more frantically, he checked every book. All of them seemed normal.

When Miss Tull showed up an hour later, Matt strolled over to her desk and asked his favorite librarian, "Is there anything special about the books on Mr. Rickets?"

"All books are special," she replied with a smile that tilted the glasses on her long nose.

"Have you read these?" Matt asked, trying to sound casual.

"Most."

"How about *The Sword and the Flute*?"

Gray eyes locked onto him over the top of her specs. "You must be mistaken," she replied. "There is no such title."

Matt showed her the book.

She frowned and said, "Hmm, I will have to enter it into the catalog. What is it about?"

Matt stepped back from this question, mumbling something about getting to class. No sense having Miss Tull concerned over his sanity. He hadn't even told his parents about what had happened.

The next few days he poked around Mr. Rickets whenever Miss Tull wasn't looking. He was dying to find a way back to the Propylon. He needed to know if Queen Bea had made it home with Ian's Flute. Were there other Talis on Earth that needed finding? Would the Sword summon him to help find them?

Evidently not.

Life went on as it had before his adventure. Eventually, Matt gave up searching for portals. However, he did decide to prepare himself in case he was called upon again. Since he was now a knight, he would learn how to handle a sword. He read books on fencing and checked into martial arts built around swordplay such as *aikido* and *kenjutsu*. He even discovered the Society for Creative Anachronism, a group that recreated medieval jousts and tournaments. Finally he settled on *Kendo*, the Way of the Sword.

No one in his family understood Matt's sudden interest in swords. His mom worried about injuries. His dad expected him to tire of the training and discipline involved. But they both knew that once Matt got an idea into his head, he was more stubborn than crabgrass. And so they signed the permission slip and bought the uniform, the body armor, and several *shinai*—bamboo practice swords.

For the next few months, Matt went to the *dojo* every day after school. He skipped indoor soccer and focused on kendo. He worked hard on his eye-hand coordination, practicing attacks and defenses as though his life depended on it.

One day it might.

The seasons worked their way around to spring. On a fresh Friday afternoon, Matt came home from school, changed clothes, grabbed his pack, and headed for The Loft. The Loft was an eight-foot-square tree house nestled in the heart of an ancient apple tree. Matt had helped Vic and his dad build it many years ago. It perched six feet off the ground, which was plenty high for Matt. Thick branches and lush leaves shielded it from prying eyes while still letting in lots of sun.

This marvel of backyard engineering had been built without pounding a single nail into the venerable tree. It had running water—a plastic jug that tipped into a bucket sink at the pull of a rope—and even a garden-level basement made by hanging tarps from floor to ground.

Matt scrambled up the ladder and plopped into a scrunchy green beanbag. He had checked out *The Sword and the Flute* to reread of his adventures with Aaron the Baron. Halfway through the book, he heard a faint hissing, like air being sucked through a tiny straw. The noise was coming from a period on the page in front of him.

The spot of ink was growing.

Matt's eyes grew bigger along with it.

A portal?

At long last!

For months Matt had dreamed of this moment. Now he panicked. Butterflies banged into each other in his stomach. Beads of sweat called an emergency meeting on his forehead. His feet wanted to head straight for his bedroom.

He had almost not returned from his first tumble into a portal. Pirates had tried to kill him and a dark spirit had almost succeeded. If he knew what was good for him, he would run to the house; he would stay put in the present where it was safe.

Why would he risk taking another plunge into the unknown?

The answer came to him with caffeine clarity.

Because the Sword of Truth was calling.

Because he was the Queen's Knight.

Because he had sworn to serve the Maker.

Because he would not ignore his destiny.

The spot on the page had grown to the size of a CD. Matt could detect the swirling; he could feel the pull. His muscles tensed in anticipation. He patted his pockets to make sure he had his quote book and harmonica. Satisfied, he pressed his palms together, tucked his head and leaned forward.

First came the tingling in his fingertips then the painless stretching.

Matt had been unwittingly sucked through his first portal and deposited in a heap of arms and legs. This time he would make a better entrance. He would somersault his body as he passed through the portal and come out the other end like a superhero.

Fat chance.

THE END